PETE

LINDA FORD

1

Circle A Ranch, 1887

The lumber for the new schoolhouse was loaded on the wagon. It was barely past noon and Pete Blake was ready to return to the Circle A Ranch. He strode into the Fort Macleod station house to inform the agent.

He stepped into the cool interior, light from outdoors slanting across the wooden floor.

A young woman stood at the wicket speaking to the agent, so Pete hung back. He'd let the young woman conduct her business before he stepped forward.

"Mr. Sharp was to meet me here. We are to be married, you see."

Pete didn't mean to listen to a conversation that was none of his business, but the way she spoke fascinated him. She talked like her tongue was stuck in the back of her mouth and her r sounded like she rolled it around before releasing it.

The man at the narrow counter gave her a flash of attention. "Mr. Sharp isn't here."

The young lady—and she was very young—glanced over her shoulder. Her gaze brushed over Pete without pausing. "Aye. I dinna think so."

Pete was used to this sort of dismissal. At least, he should have been.

He stepped aside as another man entered. A fancy dude in a suit and vest. A bob hat that looked like dirt wouldn't dare settle on it. The man looked around.

"I'm expecting a Miss MacDonald."

The young lady turned to face him. "Och aye. Eva MacDonald and that 'twould be me. And you'd be Bertram Sharp. I'm ever so glad to finally meet you."

Pete pretended to be studying a poster on the wall, but he heard every word the woman spoke. It was like listening to river water run over rocks.

"My things are there."

He guessed she meant the small trunk beside the door.

Mr. Sharp's face took on a pinched look. "You never said you had red hair. And freckles like a plague. And you don't speak English. This isn't what I expected. I'm sorry." He strode from the room. His fancy, shiny shoes clapped on the wooden platform as he hurried away.

Miss MacDonald looked like the ground had fallen out from under her feet. The agent edged back, alarmed and obviously not wanting to get involved.

Miss MacDonald clutched at her stomach and swayed. If someone didn't catch her, she was going to land face-first on the floor.

Seemed there was no one but Pete.

He hurried to her side, took her elbow and guided her to the nearest bench.

She collapsed and stared into the distance.

He didn't know her, but he knew what it felt like to be rejected over one's looks. Something a person had no control over, but it didn't seem to make a difference.

His swarthy skin had often been the cause of rejection. An orphan from birth, he didn't know what race was responsible for his coloring. Some people said there had to be a black person in his background, but Maude and John said it was more likely a Spaniard. Not that it mattered to them, they reassured him.

He studied the gal beside him. He'd expected tears. Instead, she white-knuckled her satchel.

"Do you have funds to return home?" He'd buy her a ticket if she didn't.

"I have no home to return to." Her words carried a whiff of cold air.

Homeless, rejected… poor girl. "I can give you a home." Maude and John would welcome her at the Circle A.

She turned eagerly. "You'll marry me?"

He hadn't exactly offered marriage. Truth was, he didn't even *want* to marry. That was an invitation for rejection in his opinion. His only reason for even considering that step was to please Maude and John. He'd gone so far as to do as Maude suggested and write to a young woman, Trudy, who was willing to be a mail-order bride. He'd offered to send her the fare to come west and marry. She seemed likable enough and interested in his offer. That is until she had a list of questions that included information about his racial heritage. Turns out she couldn't bring herself to marry anyone who wasn't white European. But if he took a wife home, John and Maude and the others would stop reminding him that he was the only one of the boys not married. They'd stop pressing him about Trudy. He supposed they deserved an explanation as to what happened that she suddenly wasn't interested in him. But he hadn't been able to give it. Hadn't been able to confess he'd been turned down as soon as she learned he wasn't blond and blue-eyed. Not that he was surprised. It seemed to matter greatly to a lot of people.

He needed to marry solely to make Maude and John happy. So why not this young woman? She needed someone. A marriage of convenience would solve something for both of them.

He focused his attention on the woman at his side. "You don't know me."

"Are you kind? Honest? God-fearing?"

"I believe am."

"Aye and that's enough for me. I'm that desperate." The agent leaned so far across the counter he was in danger of falling on his nose.

Pete drew Miss MacDonald to her feet. "Let's go where we can talk."

Neither of them spoke as they stepped into the sunshine. Pete glanced from side to side. Down by the tracks, a distance from the station and away from any houses, someone had placed a bench. "Let's go there." They made their way to the spot and sat side by side, an uncomfortable distance between them.

"Let's start from the beginning. My name is Pete Blake. I work on the Circle A Ranch. It's owned by John and Maude Arbuckle. John was hurt in an accident seven years ago and is in a wheelchair. That left Maude to run the place. The old cowboys wouldn't work for a woman, so she brought home six boys and taught them to be cowboys. I'm one of those six." He wasn't sure how much to tell her, but it seemed she should know as much as possible before she decided if she truly wanted to do this.

He continued. "All the other boys are married now. All except me." He sucked in a deep breath and faced her. "Maybe you're in too much shock to take note of the fact that my skin is darker than most people's. Some find that objectionable."

She raised her eyes. Blue as a deep mountain lake.

Unsettled as rushing water. Then she stilled her look. Squinted at him. "Thought 'twas the sun what made ya dark."

"Nope. It's my natural color. If you find it off-putting best to say so right off. I know nothing of my parents or family, so I don't know if it's from black, native, or a Spaniard."

Something flashed through her eyes, like a trick of the light. Her lips twitched. "Ya might have noticed that some object to my looks too." She caught a strand of hair that fell around her shoulders and pulled it forward. "Like the color of me hair." She brushed a fingertip across her nose. "Or me many freckles." Her shoulders sank. "Aye, and more."

More? "Like what?"

She shrugged. "Nothing that would concern ya."

Secrets? Well, he guessed she was entitled to a few, so long as they didn't affect anyone else.

She squared her shoulders. "My name is Eva MacDonald. I'm Scottish if ya haven't guessed. I've traveled from Pictou, Nova Scotia." She sat up taller, her chin tipped. "Birthplace of New Scotland, if'n ya didn't know."

He didn't. "Maude and John are needing a bit of help." They'd mentioned that Scotty was slowing down, and it would be good if Pete married a woman who could help. "Can you cook? Take care of a house?"

"Aye, that I can. Been doing it for my pa since Ma died four years ago."

"What does your pa think of you moving so far west?" What he really wanted to know was would she get tired of this adventure and want to go back?

"Pa died some months ago. I have nothing back there. Not even my pride."

He sat motionless, trying to think what she meant by that.

She waved a finger in the air. "But dinna mind that. It's in the past now."

"Very well. Maude has been hinting very strongly"—he chuckled—"that she could use some help around the house. Scotty is our cook. He's as old as the trees that were cut to make the house. "

She snorted at his exaggeration. Her eyes lit like the sun had peeked out from behind a cloud. "Scotty, ye say? Another Scotsman then?"

"I couldn't say. He doesn't talk like you do. Talks like an old cowboy. Maude says he needs help in the kitchen, especially preparing for Sundays. You see, everyone gathers at the house for a church service and then to share a meal."

"Everyone?"

"Remember I said Maude had brought out six boys? They are all married and have their own homes and there are now six children."

Her eyes lit at that announcement.

"I'd be willing to help Mr. Scotty."

"It's just Scotty. Would you also be willing to help Maude with housework?"

She nodded so vigorously her hair flipped back and forth.

He choked back the tightness in his throat at her innocent eagerness. "If we marry, it will only be to solve our problems."

"Aye. I'm in need of a home. And what's your problem?"

He hadn't expected her to be so direct. "I know my skin color keeps people from wanting anything to do with me." Especially, it seemed, most young ladies. He studied her, unblinkingly waiting for her decision.

She met his gaze, hers steady.

Her hair wasn't exactly red. Not like the bright color he'd seen on a man one time. Hers was more like the color of bricks. Her skin reddened beneath her freckles. He was about to apologize for staring when she spoke.

"Ya've had time to study me looks. Are ya going to be like Mr. Sharp and object?" Her eyes bored into his. She looked ready to put up her fists and demand justice for his judgment. Though he'd not given his opinion. She reminded him of something Maude had said one time when a little cockerel strutted across the yard. Something about the smaller the beast the bigger the fight. A grin tugged at his lips, but he decided it was best to keep it to himself.

"I don't object to your looks," he said soberly, sincerely. "Do you object to mine?"

Her study continued. She grinned, transforming her face to a dance of mobile freckles.

He watched, fascinated at how her emotions played so plainly on her face. He knew she would speak approval even before she opened her mouth.

"The Spaniards must be handsome as Scottish lairds." She lowered her eyes.

Pete knew nothing about Scottish lairds. Not even what they were. But the word 'handsome' was enough reason to marry her.

"I've told you about my family—those at the Circle A—now tell me a bit about yourself."

Her eyes flashed and a look of misery crossed her face so quickly he almost missed it.

"I'm sorry," he said. "I realize it hasn't been long since your father died. But do you have other family back east?"

"Och, no." She stopped. "Forgive me. I will try to speak better English."

"No need. I understand you very well."

A smile flashed across her face before she lowered her head, the curtain of brick-colored hair hiding her face. "Thank you," she whispered.

For several seconds neither of them spoke. He wasn't sure how to proceed. But he couldn't sit under the midday sun forever. "So we agree we'll marry?" He could hardly believe it was that easy.

"Aye. I will help cook and clean. I will warm your

bed if you wish." Her freckles stood out against her flushing face.

Sure, in his most remote dreams, he'd like a wife curled up next to him at night, but to welcome her into his bed would be to open his heart and he would never do that. Besides, she was a stranger. Somehow that felt wrong. And with her tousled hair, she looked like a child.

He must make something clear. "I wouldn't expect you to share my bed."

Air whooshed from her. She needn't be quite so relieved. "A marriage in name only?"

He nodded, wondering what her reaction would be.

"Can ya promise ya won't grow weary of me and send me packing?" Her gaze drilled into his, demanding…or was it begging?

"I promise I won't and I'm a man of my word. What I promise, I do to the best of my ability. And would you likewise promise you wouldn't get tired of me and run off?"

Her look softened, relaxed. "I can promise ya this. If I have a problem with ya, I will speak to ya about it. Somehow we will work things out."

"That sounds good to me."

"Aye, and to me as well. I used to believe in love and romance. Now I just want security."

"You'll find that at the ranch. How old are you?" She looked far too young to be so jaded.

She squared her shoulders and drew her chin back. "I am seventeen years old." A beat of expectant silence.

Seventeen? It seemed so young and yet he knew many, if not most, young women were married by that age. Some younger.

"How old are you?" she asked.

"I'm twenty-one." Though most days he felt a lot older.

She tipped her head from side to side and studied him. "Is everyone at your ranch as easy to get along with?"

He laughed outright. "Nope. I'm the best."

Her expression grew wary and he knew she worried about what she would encounter at the Circle A. "But the others are nice too. You'll soon see for yourself." He plopped his palms to his knees. "Are we ready to get hitched?"

"Hitched, is it now?"

Had he offended her with his off-hand remark?

AT THE WORD HITCHED, Eva felt a bubble of laughter make its way up her chest. It escaped into the air. She tried to control it, but the last few days had left her exhausted physically, emotionally and mentally. Rendered her powerless to tame her emotions.

Grinning, Pete drew her to her feet. "I'll take that as agreement."

She looked up into his face. Black eyes. Black wavy hair. Dark skin as he'd pointed out. Though it was more bronze than anything. Like she'd said, she thought he was darkened from the sun. Many of the fishermen she knew back home had faces showing signs of being outdoors.

She considered herself a fair judge of men. Less so of women, perhaps. But if she'd seen Mr. Sharp before she traveled all this way, she'd of known him to be a pompous man, full of his own importance. She saw none of that in Pete Blake. What she liked best about the man before him, was the steady, kind look in his eyes. That, and his offer to give her a home. All he asked in return was for her to help take care of a house. And not run off on him. She could promise both with her whole heart.

"Where do we go to get married?" she asked.

He chuckled. "I don't know. It isn't like I'm an old hand at this."

She laughed too. As much from nervousness as amusement.

Pete looked around. "A church I suppose. Or we could go to the fort and get the commanding officer to marry us."

"A Mountie could marry us?"

"You'd like that?"

"I would indeed." She looked toward the fort, fascinated by the log walls that blocked a view of what lay inside.

"Do you want to wait here while I make inquiries?"

"Are ya being polite or do ya wish me to say behind?" Best she finds out now if he meant to relegate her to a subservient role. She would immediately disabuse him of such a notion.

He crooked his elbow toward her. "I would appreciate your company."

"Aye, 'tis good to know." They crossed the street and made their way toward the stockade.

"And what would you have done if I asked you to wait?"

She hoped she heard humor in his voice. Because she didn't want to fight with him, but if they were to enjoy any bit of peace in their union, he must accept her for who and what she was. "I would have followed ya." She paused as he digested the information. "Aye and haven't I been told I have a wild streak about me."

His steps slowed to a halt. "How wild?"

"'Tis nothing for ya to fear. But I like to feel the wind on me face. I like to see the sky stretched above me. I like to tramp across the beach." She stopped. "Och, and there is no beach."

"Sorry about having no beach, but there are miles and miles of grass. About being wild, so long as no one is hurt, you can feel the wind, see the sky and walk the hills to your heart's content."

She might have hugged him at that moment. Except he would likely run for the hills at such boldness on her part. Best she keep her enthusiasm under control.

They continued onward.

Pete spoke. "Who said you were wild?"

"Och. 'Tis many have said it. Even"—her voice lowered and maybe cracked a wee bit—"me very own pa."

"I expect he meant it for your good."

To deny it would dishonor her pa and she couldn't do that. "Aye."

Wide, thick doors stood ajar, allowing them entrance into the fort. Before them was an open square and, in its center, a flagpole flying the Union Jack. Circling the square were various buildings. To her left, a chapel. She pointed it out to Pete. "Maybe we could get married there. Combine a church wedding and a Mountie one."

"Let's see what we can do." He pointed to a building with a sign on its front reading 'Headquarters.' A constable stood at guard.

The young constable snapped to attention and asked that they state their business. "Sir." He saluted as the commanding officer stepped from the building.

Pete explained that they wished to get married as soon as possible as he must return to the ranch this afternoon.

A few minutes later, she and Pete had been questioned as to their plans and a time had been chosen.

Thinking of the gown in her trunk that she expected to get married in, she had asked for an hour delay.

Pete arranged for her trunk to go to the hotel and for her to have a room to freshen up in.

Eva washed in the water provided, brushed the tangles from her hair and arranged it in a roll at the back of her head. She took out the dress she'd planned to marry Mr. Sharp in, smoothed it as best she could and donned it then went to wait in the lobby for Pete to return.

He stared at her when he entered the room. "You look different," was all he said.

She looked down at her dress. It was a silvery gray satin. "It 'twas my ma's dress."

"It looks nice. Are you ready?"

Her trunk was taken to the wagon parked in front. Pete handed her up to the seat and they drove to the fort. He helped her down. Aye, and wasn't it a fine thing that he did? She seemed to have lost the power to order her limbs to move.

He escorted her into the tiny church. The Mountie waited for them, resplendent in his red serge coat. A man and woman waited with him.

"I asked Joe and Bertha Jones to be here as witnesses."

"Thanks," Pete said.

Eva couldn't find her tongue. Wouldn't Pa be surprised to know she could be struck dumb?

A few minutes later, they were pronounced husband and wife.

"You may kiss the bride." The words hollowed out her head. She froze.

Pete caught her chin, turned her face toward him, and brushed his warm, firm lips over hers.

Och, and didn't her eyes feel like they were too big for their sockets? Too big to allow her eyelids to blink over them.

Pete drew her to his side as he thanked the others.

"Are you ready to travel?" he asked her.

Yes. No. She forced her brain to work. "Could I find some place to change my gown?" The September heat would render her a pool of salt water trapped in that heavy dress.

The woman who had witnessed the exchange of vows…what had Eva vowed? She couldn't remember. Except for the warning, *what God has joined together, let not man put asunder.*

She had signed her name, agreeing to a life-long union.

She was about to discover if her decision was a foolish one or not.

2

Pete helped Eva to the wagon seat then climbed up to join her. Apart from asking for a place in which to change her dress, she hadn't said a word since 'I do.'

He sat beside her, the reins in his hands, but he didn't release the brake. If she regretted her hasty choice, he'd sooner find out now than later.

"Eva, if you've changed your mind, now is the time to say so."

She jerked around to face him. Blinked twice. "Och, no. I've not changed me mind." Her accent deepened so the words sounded muddled. But he understood her clear enough. "'Tis not the future I fear."

"Then what is it, because you are obviously having second thoughts."

"'Tis all so new. Overwhelming ye might say." She shook herself. "But I'm up to pursuing a new path.

What does the Good Book say? 'Forgettin' those things which are behind and reaching forth unto those things which are before.' Aye, and that is what I mean to do." She looked around. "Are we going?"

He released the brake. "Sit back. Our future awaits."

Her gaze went from side to side as they left the fort. The wagon rumbled down the street toward the west. They were soon away from the small town and facing the rolling hills that gave way to the mountains.

She sighed. "'Tis almost as good as seeing the ocean." She lifted her face, her eyes closed. "Even the breeze is familiar though the scent 'tis different." She sucked in air for a long time, then released it in a gust. "Dry it 'tis." She shook her head, freeing much of her hair from the pins that held it a moment ago, and dug her fingers into her scalp, as if massaging the strands of hair into freedom. "Aye and 'tis a good breeze."

He laughed heartily.

She shot him a look that demanded he explain what he found funny.

He sobered, though he could feel merriment in his eyes.

"Ya find me amusing?"

"Most people complain about the wind. And here you are admiring it."

"'Tis a bonnie bit of breeze."

His grin was wide as he studied this strange creature. Soberness flattened his mouth. Now his wife.

She left off looking at him as her gaze darted to the scene before them. "Flowers. A riot of them." Her look returned to him, pleading plain in her expression. "I dinna have flowers for me wedding."

He pulled the reins and the wagon stopped. "That was an oversight on my part, but we can remedy that now." He jumped to the ground and turned to lift her down.

She practically leaped into his arms. He staggered back a step to keep his balance.

Her face was bright as she hurried to the patch of flowers where she fell on her knees and bent over to sniff the mass of white, daisy-like blossoms. He'd never before been interested in flowers, but now, for the first time, he wished he knew the names of every one and could tell her something special about them.

Instead, as he watched her, the words of a poem John had read to them several times came to mind. He wasn't sure he had the words right because he hadn't paid much attention to them. Something about *gathering flowers while ye may. Time is flying. The flower that smiles today tomorrow will be dying.*

The words clanged inside his head like a warning. Telling him that Eva was happy now. But that smile and excitement would fade like yesterday's flowers.

He pushed aside the gloomy thought. This marriage came with no expectations except their promises to each other to stick it out.

But how well he knew that promises easily given could just as easily be forgotten.

Eva sat back on her heels and lifted her face to the sky. She pocketed the last of the hairpins and shook her head. The wind blew her hair out behind her like a sail.

He chuckled softly so as to not draw attention to himself, but if it was wind she wanted, she wouldn't be disappointed.

She picked flowers for a few minutes, then rose and turned to face him. Her eyes glowed with such joy that his mouth went dry. Did it really take so little to please her? If so, he could hope she'd be happy at the ranch.

And with him?

He wasn't prepared to hope for that.

She returned to his side. "Do ya like me bouquet?" She held it up to his nose. Her eyes held his, offering more than a chance to sniff the flowers.

He lowered his gaze to the white petals and inhaled. They smelled like grass and dust. A timely warning to remember what the future promised and it wasn't roses and sweetness. Only a practical, mutually beneficial arrangement.

He wanted nothing more than that.

They returned to the wagon and proceeded on their way.

She held the bouquet like it was hot house flowers right from Toronto and sighed like life pleased her. "How far do we have to go?" she asked.

He jerked his thoughts back to the journey. "With the wagon loaded so heavily, it will probably take six hours or so."

"Oh." The little word breathed out.

"Is that concern I hear?"

"Och, no. 'Tis happiness. So long as we are traveling, I dinna have to face a bunch of strangers."

Of course, she would be worried about what she'd face.

He touched the back of her hand, surprised at its softness. Or was he surprised at the warmth that raced up his arm and shot into his heart like an arrow?

"I can put your mind at ease. You will be welcomed and, within hours, no longer a stranger."

She nodded but continued to face forward. "And won't they be surprised that ya bring home a wife when they expected ya to bring home only lumber?"

He chuckled, bringing her gaze to him. "I suppose they will be a mite surprised."

Her eyes flashed with amusement. "A mite, ye say? Pray tell, what would be considered a large surprise?"

He grinned. "Guess I don't know and maybe don't want to." With her smiling at him, he could believe there would be no surprises that would jerk the ground from beneath his feet.

Her gaze shifted to her left. "'Tis lumber for an important project?"

He didn't look to the side but kept his eyes on her. "A schoolhouse."

She jerked his attention back to him. "Is there nae a school the bairns attend?"

"There soon will be. Then we'll need a teacher."

He could see her analyzing what it meant. "Parents have been teaching the children."

She nodded. "Tell me about the children. And the parents too."

"There's Dillon and Abby. They have a baby boy. Neil." She could learn about the pair and their baby as she grew to know them. "Then there's Mike and Bethany. That's quite the story. Mike was in the orphanage until Maude took him to the ranch. Bethany is the girl his sister raised as her stepdaughter. Mike and Beth adopted Dakota from the same orphanage. The boy is seven."

"Och. Sounds romantic it does."

"Are you wishing for romance?" He heard the hard tone in his words.

"Not anymore."

"Did you expect it with Mr. Sharp?" Had the man wooed her with sweet words and big promises?

"I was daft to believe the things he said. I wanted a place where I belonged and it made me ignore things I shouldn't have ignored." She sniffed the flowers. "But then here I am now. A married woman going to a home. Isn't it what I wanted? So it has all worked out for the best. Just as the Good Book says it will."

"John and Maude will like you."

"Why do you say that?"

"Because you refer to the Good Book. You'll find that they read often from the Bible, know many verses by heart, and conduct a service every Sunday."

"'Tis good to know. Now aren't there more than two young men you need to tell me about?"

He liked how her 'about' sounded like aboot. "There's more for sure. "Noah and Lainie. He found her squatting on Circle A Ranch land with her sister and brother. Missy is seven, Boyd is twelve. Lainie refused to leave until her campsite was washed away." He grinned as he thought of their courtship. "Then there's Adam and Grace. Grace, Sam's sister, was adopted by a family. Sam married Yvette, Grace's friend. It's Yvette's father who purchased the materials for the schoolhouse. And last, but not least, there is me."

"And me. Pete and Eva."

He touched the back of her hand again. "Yes, Pete and Eva."

She gave him a sober look. "May God bless us both. Amen."

Their looks locked. Her gaze sought truth and something more from him. He didn't know what she wanted. Nor if he could give it, but he'd promised 'til death do them part and he meant it. "We'll let God do the blessing, but we'll do the living of it." He didn't know if she'd understand what he meant. Only that they had to make the effort to make this work.

"Aye, and that I will do."

"And I."

Their promise settled into Pete's heart and put down roots.

Eva jumped to her feet. "Och. Look at the wee cows."

The wagon hit a bump and she was thrown off balance.

Eva tipped toward the ground. She should have known better than to stand up simply because she saw some cows in the distance. Mixed brown and black and white animals grazing in the straw-colored grass. Aye, 'twas a sight to behold but she should have stayed seated.

Pete's big hand grabbed her arm and pulled her back to the seat. He didn't say anything but kept his hand firmly on her arm.

She swallowed hard, waiting for him to voice his displeasure. But her heart had stopped its furious racing and he still didn't say anything. "That was a foolish thing to do," she said in her most humble tone.

Nothing. Not a word. Was he so angry he couldn't speak? And what did he do with his anger? Perhaps she should have considered that question before she tied her life to his. Nothing for it now but to face his wrath.

She turned. "Pete, I am sorry."

He faced forward. Didn't turn despite her plea.

"Pete, are you angry? Say something. Do something." She'd sooner deal with his anger now than have it hanging over her head, constantly wondering when he'd express it. That's how her father had been.

He sucked in air and turned toward her. "I am not mad, but you did give me a scare. I'm glad you didn't get thrown out."

"You're not angry?" She couldn't fathom the idea.

He cupped his hand over hers where it lay on her knee, still clutching the wildflowers she'd picked. A gentle smile curved his mouth. "I don't fancy getting married and widowed on the same day. Nor do I wish to see you hurt."

Tears erupted from her eyes. She ducked her head, knowing her face would be twisted and her freckles standing out like beacons from a lighthouse. Despite her best efforts, a sob escaped.

The wagon stopped moving.

"Eva, what's wrong?"

She couldn't answer. Couldn't speak around the tears and tightness gripping her heart.

His hands clasped her shoulders and he eased her back, one curled finger caught under her chin and he tipped her face up.

"Why are you crying? What have I done?"

Embarrassed about her tears, she couldn't meet his gaze.

"Eva, tell me what I've done wrong so I can make it right."

Without her consent, her gaze went to his. The concern in his eyes was her undoing. "Ya've done nothing wrong. I thought you'd be angry."

"I'm not."

"My father was angry with me so often. For days he'd let me wait for his punishment. I hated that. I'd sooner he'd whipped me or shut me in the cellar than give me the silent treatment."

"He whipped you? Shut you in the cellar?"

"Only when I deserved it," she whispered.

His arms came around her and he pulled her to his chest. His heart beat beneath her cheek. His warmth filled her heart.

"No one deserves such harsh punishment. No one." His voice rumbled from his chest.

She took comfort in his words and embrace, but she also heard something in his tone. For a few seconds, she remained sheltered in his arms, then eased back.

He dropped his arms, looked away, and cleared his throat.

She understood his embarrassment. Shared it even. But she wouldn't allow it to stop her from responding to what her heart had heard.

She caught his chin and turned him toward her.

"You too have known harsh punishment. I heard it in yer voice." She thought of the words *as deep calleth unto deep*. Or in this case, as heart calleth unto heart.

His gaze found hers and she saw a pain in his eyes that came from his depths.

"Tell me what happened."

He cleared his throat again. "Whippings were common in the orphanage. We even had what we called the whipping chair. We held to the back or the arms depending on our size while the mister gave vent to his wrath."

She understood the pain from those experiences still dwelled in his heart. She could do no less than offer him the same comfort he'd given her and she slipped her arms around his waist and hugged him.

At first, he was stiff, unresponsive and then he melted into her embrace. For several heart beats they held each other.

She cou'nae speak for him, but to find someone who understood how it felt to be treated so harshly felt like something in her heart had been smoothed over with a healing balm. She withdrew her arms and sat back, hoping her actions wouldn't have offended him.

He picked up the reins and they resumed their journey.

For a few miles, neither of them spoke. But she'd never been one to keep her thoughts to herself. "'Twould seem we have something in common."

"You mean besides being married to each other?"

She heard the teasing in his tone and laughed. "Aye, and I won't be forgetting that."

"I'll remind you if you do."

They'd climbed a steep hill and began a descent on the other side. "We'll take a break here and let the horses rest," he said.

They drew up beside a stream of clear blue water. She barely waited for her feet to touch the ground before she rushed to the flowing brook, fell on her stomach and trailed her fingers in the cold liquid. It rushed by her, gurgling like laughter.

Pete led the horses to water and then squatted beside Eva. He filled the canteen.

She cupped water to her mouth, delighting in the cool freshness, then sat up. "'Tis so different to think of drinking the water. And to see it laughing by rather than lapping at my feet."

"I've never seen the ocean," he said.

"'Tis a marvelous sight. Disappearing into the horizon. Moody as an old woman. One day it is calm, splashing at yer feet like a watery tease. The next day, roaring with waves that would suck ya into its depths." She sat beside him, her thoughts on her memories. "My pa was a fisherman. His boat capsized in one of the storms. He was the only one that drowned. No one else." Her head fell forward. "They blamed me," she whispered.

"Blamed you for the storm?"

"No. For Pa's drowning." She faced Pete, needing to see his reaction. "They said if I was a better daughter the sea wou'nae taken him."

Pete's forehead furrowed. "I don't understand. How are the two related?"

"The Good Book says 'For rebellion is as the sin of witchcraft.' Because I preferred to feel the wind and the sun and the sand to staying home and stoking the fire, many called me rebellious." A knife slashed at her heart, attacking wounds that never quite healed. Her voice again fell to a whisper. "So I was to blame for God not protecting Pa."

Pete burst to his feet. "That's one of the dumbest things I've ever heard. Have these people never read where it says, 'Whither shall I flee from thy presence? If I ascend up into heaven, thou art there: if I make my bed in hell, behold, thou art there. If I take the wings of the morning and dwell in the uttermost parts of the sea; even there shall thy hand lead me, and thy right hand shall hold me.'? That too is in the Good Book."

Eva stood and looked up at him. "'The uttermost parts of the sea?'"

He nodded. "Even there God was with him."

"Then why did he drown?" It seemed there had to be someone or something to blame.

"I don't know. Any more than I know why babies die, or why floods and fires take people's homes." He leaned closer, his intent look making it impossible for her to turn away. "But this I know with all my heart—

God did not punish you for enjoying the wind, the sun, and the sand. All are His good gifts. I think He would be displeased if we didn't enjoy His gifts."

Afraid he would think she meant to spend her time wandering the hills, she spoke up. "I won't be wasting my time at the ranch enjoying such foolishness. I've agreed to do a job and I will."

He caught her hand and tugged her after him. They trotted to a little rise that allowed her to see to the west. "See the mountains?"

"I could hardly miss 'em."

"That's right. But you could keep your eyes on the ground. The mountains would still be there but you have to look up to enjoy them."

Her gaze drank in the sight of them. "Never seen anything like this back east."

"Well, don't waste the sight of them by keeping your eyes on the ground."

Understanding his meaning, she laughed. "Pete, it seems that yer a philosopher."

He lifted his hands in protest. "Not at all. Please never say that in front of the others. Besides, I'm just telling you the facts."

"That I can enjoy the view while tending to chores?" She hesitated a moment then added what she thought he meant. "And I can be a proper young lady and still enjoy the wind and the sky?"

He grinned. "That's right."

She couldn't tear herself from his gaze and he

didn't seem inclined to look away. A strand of her hair blew across her face and she pushed it back. "I'll do my best to keep my hair tied back."

"Why?"

"Och and isn't it proper and all?"

He reached out and pulled a handful of hair over her shoulder. "If letting the wind blow it is what gives you pleasure then let it fly free." He released her hair and stepped back. "I brought some food. Let's eat while the horses rest."

She followed him to the wagon, where he pulled out a sack and divided cheese, hunks of bread, and dill pickles between them, then handed her an apple. They sat side by side against one of the wagon wheels to eat.

"Pete, ya are a strange man."

She felt shock race through his body and instantly perceived he'd taken her words to mean something other than what she intended. Before those careless words had time to wound him, she caught his hand. "Not in the way ya think I mean. But because ya could be asking many things of me. How I wear me hair? What I do with me time? But no. Ya dinna do that. If it's what you really mean, then I consider myself blessed to have found you." As was often her problem, she had blurted out words without considering their effect. He would no doubt consider her brash, forward, a woman with an untamed tongue.

She felt his stillness; as if every muscle in his body

had frozen. She wondered if even his heart continued to beat.

Her own breath caught in her lungs, a painful knot of fear and uncertainty.

Would she now learn how he dealt with her waywardness?

3

Pete couldn't form a decent thought. Blessed, she'd said. And she meant him. But what did she know? She'd met him only a few hours ago. Wait until she'd known him days, weeks, months... no point in saying years. He couldn't believe her tune wouldn't change in time. Though he would do everything possible to make her happy.

Feeling her stillness, remembering how she'd previously worried what his reaction would be, he forced his worries aside so he could respond to her statement. "Eva, you are not my prisoner, nor are you my servant. We have an agreement. You help Maude and Scotty. In return, you have a home and security. With that arrangement, I consider myself fortunate." He couldn't bring himself to say blessed. "It's mutually beneficial."

"So ya say, but 'tis more so for me than ye."

"I guess that's for me to say."

She shifted so she faced him, the half-eaten apple in one hand. "I like our arrangement so far."

"Good. Now let's be on our way." He was slow to get to his feet. They seemed in such accord here. But they must continue on.

They returned to the wagon and resumed their journey.

Eva's gaze darted from side to side, her expression eager, as if she couldn't see enough of the country. After a bit, she moved less. Her head drooped. It appeared she'd fallen asleep. He shifted so she leaned against his shoulder. She was obviously exhausted and no wonder. The journey from Nova Scotia would have taken her many days. He'd let her sleep as long as she liked, and there'd be no objection on his part for her using him for a pillow.

The rough trail threatened to put her off balance, so he slipped his arm around her and held her steady.

She sighed and put her hands under her cheek, her knuckles pressing into his chest.

A feeling he'd never before experienced filled him. He tried to figure out what it was. As his wife, he would make sure Eva had all she needed and wanted. So the feeling had a taste of protectiveness. But that didn't explain it completely. Her easy acceptance of him felt good. Her promise to never leave filled him with hope, although it carried an uncertainty to it. Promises easily given were just as easily forgotten. He might need to remind himself of that fact over and over in order to protect himself. After all, leaving didn't hurt near as much if he expected it and prepared himself for it.

Finally, he allowed himself to circle in on the most prominent feeling. She'd said she was blessed to have found him. Although he wasn't ready to believe she'd always feel that way, he liked that she'd felt free to say it to him. *Blessed.*

Once before he'd known someone who'd said that. Maybe this time it really would be true. Not that he meant to count on it. He could fulfill his promises to Eva without opening his heart to that sort of pain.

She jerked and stilled.

He guessed she'd wakened but she made no move to sit up. And he didn't let her know he was aware that she was awake.

They rode that way for several minutes, then she straightened, stretched, and yawned. "I fell asleep."

"I guess you were tired."

"Aye, 'twas a long trip."

"Did Mr. Sharp send you fare for a sleeper car?"

"Och, no, just a ticket. I'm surprised he didn't ask for the return of the fare."

Pete chuckled. "Maybe he forgot."

"I dinna think the man would forget a penny if he dropped it down a grate. No, 'tis more likely he wanted to get away from me for fear I would insist on the wedding he promised."

Before Pete could get a word of sympathy out, Eva laughed.

"Aye, and lucky he is. Luckier am I though." She sat back. "How long did I nap?"

"Not long." Her flowers had fallen and he gathered them up and handed them to her.

Their gazes caught and held. Hers exploring, going deep…looking for something. He couldn't imagine what she sought or he would offer it. If he could.

She shifted away, freeing him from her probing look. "Tell me where everyone lives. At this ranch, we're bound for."

He was relieved to be able to talk about something less emotional. "John and Maude live in the big house that they built when they first came here. Except it is the second house they built. Dillon and Abby live in the log cabin that was their first home. Then there are three new cabins. One each for Mike and Bethany, Adam and Grace, and Sam and Yvette." She was keeping track of the couples on her fingers.

"That's only four," she said when he hesitated.

"Noah and Lainie have a house a distance from the others."

She digested the information. "Why?"

"Why what?"

"Why are Noah and Lainie a distance away?"

"That was their choice. I guess Noah always thought of living on that piece of land. It's within easy walking distance."

"Aye, 'tis like back home. Everyone livin' close. Close enough to know everyone's business. A body couldn't change their mind but what everyone knew." She let out a long-suffering sigh. "It was like being stitched in a tightly-knitted muffler." She pulled an imaginary scarf around her neck.

"You sound like you don't care for it." That could be a problem. "It has its advantages."

"Aye, and what would they be?"

"There's always someone to talk to."

"Och and if ya crave some peace and quiet?"

He chuckled and pointed to her right and then to his left. "March yourself off in any direction and you can be alone."

Her gaze slowly circled and then came to him. "Aye, and is it that simple?"

"I think so. It appears to me that the women folk visit when they want but respect each other's privacy." He let that soak in. "It seems to me that you are expecting it to be crowded. It isn't that way."

She nodded, her eyes still dark and uncertain.

"Eva, what happened to you back east to make you so fearful of people?"

"I told you. 'Tis hurtful to be judged unkindly."

"And don't I know it?"

Her gaze swept his cheeks.

He didn't flinch. She'd known what he was, or rather what he wasn't, when they married. Not that he didn't realize there would be times she would be embarrassed at his coloring.

She touched his cheek. "Aren't we the bonnie pair? Both judged for our looks. And in my case, my actions too. D'ya think God brought us together to heal each other's hurts?"

He caught her hand and squeezed it gently. "That would be nice."

The air between them was heavy with unfamiliar feelings. He guessed she felt it too. For she withdrew her hand and faced forward.

He was grateful to be free of her inquisitive look so he could sort out his thoughts. Was it possible that God had brought them together? Two young adults who were tried and found wanting because of looks. Though, if he hadn't seen it for himself, he would never have guessed someone would object to Eva's looks. Fresh as the morning sunshine. Her face brightened with every good thought. Her eyes darkened when she thought of the unkindnesses she'd endured.

I will never speak unkindly to her.

He remembered her vow. If she had a problem, she would talk to him about it. Find a way to work things out.

No reason they couldn't make this work. More than that. They could make it a pleasant arrangement for both of them.

The little town of Logan Crossing came into view. He might as well introduce Eva to Abner and Ilsa.

She was already perched on the edge of the seat, her eyes on the few buildings.

"It's our nearest town. Logan Crossing. Remember I told you about Mike?"

She nodded without shifting her gaze from the buildings ahead of them.

"You recall I told you his sister raised a young woman?"

"Beth I think. She married Mike. Maybe?"

"That's correct. Well, his sister Ilsa married the storekeeper, Abner George. We'll stop and say hello."

Eva sat back so hard the wagon seat jostled. He looked at her. Her eyes were wide. Her freckles standing out against her pale skin. She looked about ready to pass out.

"Are you all right?" He grabbed her arm just in case.

"Aye. But am I ready to meet yer friends? Nae."

He slowed the wagon and faced her squarely. "Eva, you are my wife. I expect you to be treated with kindness and respect. I know Ilsa will welcome you." He wasn't sure he could say the same for Abner. The man could be dour and dismissive at times. But should he say anything offensive to Eva, Pete would make it clear it wouldn't be tolerated.

Her shoulders went back. Her chin went up. Her eyes flashed. He couldn't say what she was feeling but knew if she had fears, she meant to ignore them and deal with what lay ahead.

"I know what it's like to face an unknown. Three

times I was taken from the orphanage to strangers. I didn't know what I'd encounter. At first, I wanted to believe it would be good. All my dreams and wishes come true. But I quickly discovered it was not to be, and I learned to bury any thought of belonging as soon as it came. I found people who treated their dog better than they treated a brown boy."

Her hand clasped his. "Och. I'm sorry to hear of such people."

He turned his hand to hers. "I can assure you that you will be treated well here. My friends are nothing but kind."

"I believe you."

"What is it?" he asked when she didn't look away.

"'Tis nothing, except I hope they treat you well too."

"They do. The Circle A Ranch is a good place."

"Then dinna ya think we should be on our way?" Her eyes sparkled with teasing.

He laughed. "Mrs. Blake, I think you are looking forward to this adventure."

"Adventure, aye." He'd called her Mrs. Blake. She was now a married woman. It was what she'd wanted when she left Pictou. It ha'nae turned out the way she'd planned. But Pete—her husband—she turned the word around in her thoughts a time or two—Pete offered her a home. A safe home. He'd said he expected his friends to treat her well. Dinna it feel like God had smiled at her? And wou'nae her own friends be all twisted about to know that Pete thought she deserved kindness?

But her nerves tingled as the town drew closer.

"Tiny town," she murmured. The trail ran through town and into the distance with barely a nod at buildings on either side. Couldn't be more than twenty people lived along the dusty street.

"Just the essentials. The blacksmith shop." Pete nodded in that direction. "He also owns the livery barn. In those houses are people you might meet someday." He indicated the dwelling behind the places of business, then drew to a stop in front of a building that bore a sign. *George's General Store*.

"This is it," Pete said.

"Aye, 'tis." She tried to sound excited but knew she failed when Pete squeezed her hand.

"Eva, stick close to me. I'll make sure no one hurts you."

"Aye, you'll protect me from the monsters then?"

He chuckled. "I shall." He helped her down and smiled at her. "Everyone is going to love you."

Heat raced up her neck. She knew her cheeks would blaze red as a torch. Love was not part of their agreement and she was'nae so foolish as to dream of it.

She smoothed her skirt, pulled her hair back and

jabbed in a few hairpins before she filled her lungs with dry, dusty air and faced the store. "I'm ready."

He crooked his arm and she put her hand around his elbow to rest on his forearm. Took comfort in the strength she felt beneath her palm.

Together they climbed the steps and entered the interior of the store. She breathed in scents. Some familiar. Jute from ropes. Linseed oil. Other scents she couldn't identify. If she was on her own she'd explore, but a man stepped from a doorway behind the counter.

"Pete. Wasn't expecting ya. Ilsa," he called over his shoulder. "It's Pete." The man squinted at Eva. "And a woman."

A pretty woman with light brown hair and blue eyes joined the man behind the counter.

"Pete, nice to see you," she said in a far more welcoming voice than the man.

Pete drew Eva forward. "Abner, Ilsa, I'd like you to meet my wife. Eva, this is Mr. and Mrs. George who own the store."

Eva didn't know if she should offer her hand or curtsy.

"Yer married?" The surprise in Mr. George's voice turned Eva's tongue to dust and her limbs to wood. She could neither speak nor move.

"Abner!" Mrs. George scolded her husband. She reached for Eva's hand. "Congratulations. I wish you all the best."

"Thank you," Eva murmured, doing her best to speak plain English without the accent she'd used all her life. A kind lady on the train ride had tutored her in how to correct her speech.

"Come in for tea and tell us how you met," Mrs. George said.

Eva's insides shriveled at the invitation. She and Pete should have discussed how they were going to explain their sudden marriage.

"We can only stop a moment. I need to get home." Pete placed a hand at Eva's back and guided her past the counter into the quarters beyond. "Let me handle this," he whispered.

She looked around at the pleasant living area. It was not unlike the home she'd left in Nova Scotia, except there was no oilcloth jacket or smelly footwear. No peacoat tossed across a chair. No mishmash of papers, tobacco, and old coffee cups scattered over the table. She'd grown used to the untidiness of her home. Pa had bellowed if she moved anything of his. To see the neatness here lifted a burden in her heart. Maybe this was how people in the west lived. If so, she might be tempted to think she'd found a tiny corner of heaven.

The four of them sat at the table. Pete took the chair next to her. She could have hugged him at that moment to know he was sticking to her side.

Mrs. George made tea and served it with cookies.

Pete kept the conversation going by talking of the

lumber in the wagon and plans for the schoolhouse. Thankfully, Eva wasn't expected to add anything to that discussion.

But as soon as a break came, Mrs. George leaned forward. "I'm so glad Pete has finally married. We all feared he might not."

Eva nodded.

"I said I would when the time was right. We just had to choose when and where." Pete made it sound like he'd been planning this for a long time.

Feeling her cheeks warm, she ducked her head.

Pete continued. "I believe we suit each other." He drained his cup. "Now we must be on our way. Thank you for the refreshment."

He pulled out Eva's chair and drew her hand around his crooked elbow.

The Georges followed them to the wagon and waved goodbye as they drove away.

The town disappeared in their dust as they rolled down the trail.

Eva's lungs relaxed. She sat back, at ease for the first time since they approached the town.

"It wasn't so bad, was it?" Pete asked.

"What will ya tell others about how we met?"

"What do you want them to know?"

She considered the question. "I'm na good at keeping things to meself."

"So what do you suggest we say?"

"I dinna know. Do ya want to say ya found me

abandoned at the station and took pity on me?" She meant to be teasing but couldn't bring a smile to her lips.

"Why don't I say something like what I told Ilsa? That we decided we suited each other?"

She considered the words. Even more, she considered how he said them with such surety. As if he believed them. She tucked the thought into a little corner of her heart where it would be safe. Where she could take it out from time to time and enjoy it again. "I like that."

"Good." He squeezed her hand. "I don't feel we have to explain everything about ourselves."

"So we'll not tell them about the station and Mr. Sharp?"

He looked into her eyes, searching deep. "If it's something you want to tell, go ahead. It's up to you."

His dark eyes had the power to settle her nerves, calm her thoughts and make her think clearly.

"Och, no. I'll keep that little bit of news to myself." She chuckled. "Lest they think we're both daft."

His gaze still held hers, but now it held uncertainty. "Is that what you think? That we're crazy?"

She heard what he didn't say. Did she have to be daft to marry a man like him? And he wasn't thinking because they had just met. She touched his hand. "Pete, it might be daft to marry so quickly but it's smart to know a good man when you see one." She squeezed his hand. "And I believe I see one."

Emotion burned in the depths of his eyes. She knew her words had pleased him.

Aye, wasn't it good to know she could bring pleasure with her words? She'd do her best to continue to do so.

"Poor Mr. Sharp," Pete said.

"Poor Mr.—"She sputtered.

Pete laughed like he enjoyed Eva's surprise. "Yes, indeed. The man doesn't know that he let a sweet gal like you escape."

She lost herself in the approval in his eyes and of his words. Could it be possible that they had found what they each longed for? Someone who approved of them? Looks, words and all.

"See now." Pete pointed. "Off in the distance, you get a glimpse of the ranch."

She strained forward. There were buildings in the distance, but she couldn't see them well enough to take stock of them. She made out a flash of blue from a thread of water, a green strip of trees and then the trail dipped and she could see it no longer.

"We'll soon be there." Pete's words were calm, soothing as if he knew the rolling unsettledness of her insides.

"Aye, and then what?"

He patted her hand where it lay on her leg, curled into a knot of nerves. "Then everyone will get to meet my wife."

His tone said that was a good thing.

She sucked back her uncertainty. There was no reason this couldn't work.

At least no reason she was aware of and it hit her in the middle of her stomach that there were many things she had yet to discover.

"God, help and guide us as He has promised in His word."

4

God help us? As if the future threatened like a storm. Pete's first reaction was to be offended, then he switched direction in his thoughts. Of course, she was nervous, but she'd made it clear she chose to be with him and had not yet found a reason to regret her decision.

"I will do my best to make sure you won't be sorry for this choice," he said.

Her gaze came slowly to him. Blue and turbulent. Then the storm calmed. "And I will do the same."

It was enough for him. Perhaps enough for her too.

The trail turned to the north, avoiding the rocks ahead. To ease Eva's worries, he pointed out landmarks. The big rock where a man had fallen and broken his arm. "Before our time," he added. "And the man was only accepting a dare that said he couldn't climb it." He indicated a bunch of trees. "There's an owl nest there. A great horned owl."

"Will we see the bird?"

"We might." But they passed the site without any sign of it.

They turned south again, approaching the last hill before they descended into the valley where the ranch buildings were.

He drew to a halt when they could see the houses and barn. "There it is. Home."

She drew in a sharp breath and held it as she studied the view. After a second or two, she released her air. "'Tis bigger than Logan Crossing."

"I guess it is. That's the big house to the left where we'll live. You can pick out the barn. The row of smaller structures is sheds—harness shop, storage. Next is Scotty's cabin. Then—"

"I thought Scotty lived in the big house."

"He's always had his own place. Says he needs to have some peace and quiet." He continued his list. "There's the bunkhouse, which is only used when we have a temporary crew in. Then three cabins, as I said, for the married couples. You can't see Noah's place." He pointed out the corrals, the horses, the chicken house, and the garden.

She sat so still he wondered if she'd forgotten to breathe.

"Eva? What do you think?" He touched her shoulder and she jolted.

"It's all the Circle A Ranch?"

"Those are only the ranch buildings. Our lease goes far to the south and west."

Her eyes were wide as she looked at him. "But 'tis so big."

"Eva, it's home and that's what matters."

Her eyes narrowed. "Aye, that's all that matters."

They continued onward, driving down the gentle slope to the valley and approaching the buildings from the east.

John and Maude sat on the veranda where they often spent the evening hours. They had blankets over their knees against the evening cool. Dusk filled the hollows behind the house. The promise of sunset turned the western sky pink.

Pete wondered if Eva even noticed. Her breath rasped in and out. Her hands gripped the last few flowers so hard she choked the life from them.

He would normally have taken the wagon directly to the barn to unload the lumber and take care of the horses, but today he drove to the front of the house.

"Whoa." He didn't move to get down as Maude and John looked at him and his passenger with barely disguised surprise.

"Glad you made it back safely," John called.

"And you've brought company. How nice." Maude added. "Bring your friend in and introduce us."

Pete realized he'd forgotten to move. He set the brake, jumped down, and reached up to help Eva. Her gaze begged him not to leave her. He smiled and mouthed the words, "I'll be right here."

He drew her up the steps to face John and Maude. "I'd like you to meet my wife, Eva. Eva, this is John and Maude, the owners of the ranch." He saw surprise flash across Maude's face before she smiled. Of course, she expected he would bring Trudy to the ranch as his wife. One of these days, he would explain that Trudy had refused him. But not yet. Let Eva find her place here first. Her rightful place as his wife.

He hoped Eva didn't catch Maude's slight hesitation before she uttered a sincere, "Welcome."

"You've chosen a good man," John said. His words eased the tension from Pete. "Welcome to our home and family."

Eva gave a little curtsy. "I'm very pleased to meet you." She straightened, clasped her hands in front of her and said, "I've come prepared to help you both as best I can and Mr. Scotty. Can I bring ya tea or something?"

Pete read the level of her nervousness in the way her words grew more accented and the way her freckles stood out like flashing lights.

Maude lay her hands on top of Eva's. "I appreciate your offer to help. Heaven knows poor old Scotty is finding the work a bit much at times. But there is no rush. Get settled in and rested."

Scotty came from the kitchen. Pete thought he

might have already gone to his cabin, but it was good he hadn't. This way, Eva could meet him right off.

"Did I hear my name?" he asked.

Pete introduced Eva to him. "My wife."

Scotty's eyebrows rose, wrinkling his forehead even more than usual. "I thought you went to get lumber. Don't recall anyone sayin' anythin' about a wife."

"I'm sure I'm a surprise to everyone." Eva again curtsyed. "I was just saying I'm here to help ya, Mr. Scotty."

"Ain't no Mr. Scotty around here. Just me. Plain old Scotty. And I'll be grateful for the help of a pretty young thing like you." He cackled like he'd made a good joke.

Eva's cheeks blossomed pink, but she smiled. "I hope ya're saying as much after ya see how I do."

"Supper is over, but I expect he didn't feed you well." Scotty gave Pete a look that suggested Pete couldn't manage to take care of a mosquito. "There's food left over from supper. Sit yerselves down and I'll rustle up something."

"Come in. Come in." Maude shepherded them through the door and into the warm kitchen. John rolled in after them.

Eva clung to Pete's arm. A shiver raced from her to him. She might be cold, but he guessed it was more than that. She was no doubt feeling overwhelmed. Frightened even.

"I'll take her things up to our room first," he said. He tried to free himself from her grasp, but she wasn't letting him go and followed him back to the wagon. He could carry the small trunk on his own, but she grabbed the handle on one end.

"I'll help."

The look in her eyes—part anxiety, part determination—made him think there would be no point in arguing.

He led the way as they crossed the kitchen and climbed the stairs, then into the first bedroom on the left which was his. They lowered the trunk to the floor and he stood back, letting her take stock of her surroundings.

"This is my room. Now our room."

There were two beds. Her gaze went from one to the other. Her hands knotted.

His throat threatened to close off, but he managed to squeeze out a few words. "One bed can be yours and the other mine." He coughed, rubbed his neck, and forced out some more strangled words. "Unless you'd sooner have one of the other rooms."

She sucked in so hard she about emptied the room of air. "No. Best they think we are happily married."

Her words hit his solar plexus. "You're unhappy?"

She dismissed his question with a flick of her hand. "Of course not. But ya know what I mean. We agreed to be married in name only, dinna we?"

"We did."

"Aye then. I prefer not to invite questions. People can be judgmental and cruel."

"I don't care what they think. At least not on my account. But if it will keep others from judging you, then we'll not give them any reason to speculate. As long as you're comfortable with this arrangement."

She looked around the room, then sat on the edge of the bed. "Aye, strangely enough, I am. I like the idea of you this close. Makes me feel…" She doesn't finish.

He waited. "I hope it makes you feel safe."

She nodded. "Aye, it does that."

He could tell that wasn't all. "What else?"

She shrugged. "Not sure I can find the word for what I'm feeling, but I'll try. I'm a wee bit afraid of what lies ahead, but here"—she patted the bed—"I feel like I belong. Is that what getting married does to one?"

"I can't speak for what others feel, but I'm glad you feel that way."

"What about ya? How does it make you feel?"

He sat on the edge of his bed. Their knees were only inches apart. He had to confess it felt strange to think of a young woman sharing his room, being close enough he could reach out and touch her while she slept. But it also felt—"Good. It feels good." Like something he'd waited for all his life.

"Aye, then where should I put my belongings?"

He was on his feet. "Let me empty out two drawers. There's room in the wardrobe for you to hang things."

He moved his socks and other things into two drawers, leaving two empty.

She lifted the lid on her trunk and carried over neatly folded items.

He moved items from the top of the dresser to make room for her things. "I don't know why I keep these." A locket with only one side of the heart still intact, a rock with flecks of gold in it, and a child's picture book.

She settled her things in the top drawer then took the rock from his palm. "Shiny. Is it gold?"

"One might think so, but it's only fool's gold."

Her gaze drilled into his. "Aye, and is there a lesson in that?"

"I suppose there is. I found this at one of the homes I went to. Oh, I didn't steal it. It was out in the hills. I showed it to the mister and he laughed at me. 'Don't be fool enough to fall for false hope,' he said. "I've never forgotten that."

"The Good Book says, 'Hope deferred maketh the heart sick.'"

He nodded as old, familiar feelings twisted his heart. "It was one of the places I thought would become permanent. I soon learned otherwise." His words tasted like bile.

"Och, but that's not the end of things. The Book also says, 'But when the desire cometh, it is a tree of life.'" She touched his cheek. "I might not be what ya'd dreamed of, but I'm here to stay. Surely, there is something to be happy about in that."

He nodded, his heart lightened by her promise.

She turned back to the items in his hand. "A bairn's storybook? Is it something from your past?"

"No. I found it on the trail one day. Seemed a shame to let it go to waste."

"Aye, and methinks it signifies something to do with your dream." She didn't give him a chance to agree or deny but picked up the broken locket. "And did you find this?"

He'd thought he could look at the bit of jewelry without his memories rushing back like a turbulent river. He tossed the items to the side.

"I'm sorry to stir up sorrow," she murmured.

"It's nothing. Silly memories is all."

"Aye. Memories can kick a person when they're down."

The roll and gentleness of her words calmed his thoughts and drove the memories into the back room where they belonged.

She put more things in her assigned drawers, then opened the doors on the wardrobe. She pulled out his dress shirt and held it up as if examining it. She returned it to the closet then took three dresses from the trunk and hung them. One was the silvery gown she'd worn to their wedding. One was a dark green. He didn't know what the fabric was, but it looked lighter than the silver one. The third was light blue with a smattering of flowers.

"That one suits you." He hadn't meant to speak the thought aloud.

She slowly turned to face him. "How's that?"

"It's bright and cheerful. Just like you." Heat crept up his neck. He hoped she wouldn't notice.

She chuckled. "Why, I believe ya've paid me a compliment. And I thank ya."

"You're welcome." They studied each other for a moment. He liked what he saw. As he'd said, a cheerful, bright person. This arrangement might not be the fulfillment of his dreams, but it promised to be good, nonetheless.

She put away some dark skirts and colored tops, then took a big Bible from the trunk and put it on top of the dresser. "It belonged to me father." She added a brush, comb, and hand mirror.

Then, with her face a fiery red, she put a white garment under the pillow of her bed. He guessed it was her nightgown and his own cheeks warmed.

"I'm done." She sat on the side of the bed.

He again sat facing her. "Are you satisfied with this arrangement?"

"Aye." Her eyes bored into his. "Are ya?"

He reached for her hands. "I think we'll do just fine."

Sounds of the others downstairs reminded him of the meal and questions awaiting him.

"Are ya hungry?" she asked.

"Starving. Shall we go eat?" He rose and held out a hand to her.

"Aye. Wou'nae want you to perish."

For a moment they stood where they were, in the space between the two beds, facing each other. Her eyes filled with softness that caught in his eyes and sank toward his heart.

Hand in hand, they descended. Maude and John were at the table waiting.

Eva's hand tightened on his. "We are about to face the inquisition," she murmured.

"Together we stand."

"Aye."

IT WAS all Eva could do not to choke the life from Pete's hand. Surely, they must know that Pete had only met her today. Would they question her motives? Even go so far as to send her back to the fort…or wherever they thought a person like her should go. What sort of person was she then? The one her neighbors had accused her of being? Untamed and dangerous. Or the person her pa thought her to be? Useless, a nuisance. Or would they see the person she was and wanted to be? A kind, loyal woman capable of doing good things.

She vowed she would prove to them that she was all that.

Pete drew her to a chair and held it for her as she sat at the table.

He sat next to her, providing her with comfort and strength to face these people. Strangers to her but friends and family to Pete. For his sake, she would answer their questions and concerns.

"Food's ready. Eat it or I'll give it to the dog," Scotty said.

His words jerked her attention to him. He sounded gruff. Short-tempered. Much as Pa had been.

Pete chuckled. "He says that all the time. It's his way of saying he made it for us and hopes we'll enjoy it."

Scotty harrumphed but winked at her.

Her breath eased out. Teasing she didn't mind.

"I'll ask the blessing," John said. "Father in heaven, thank you for providing a wife for Pete. Thank you for Eva. May she and Pete know the joys of love and caring. Thank you for providing all our needs, including the food. Amen."

For a moment, Eva couldn't lift her head, couldn't face the others. Was John really thankful that she was Pete's wife? How could he be when he didn't know the first thing about her? For all he knew, she could be one of those black widow women that her neighbor had told her about.

"Eva?"

Pete's gentle voice pulled her back to her situation. He held a bowl of mashed potatoes toward her.

Her mouth flooded with saliva as she realized how hungry she was and how good the food smelled. There was rich brown gravy for the potatoes, slices of roast beef, and a medley of carrots, green beans, and peas. She took a few bites then set her fork down.

"Scotty, 'tis wonderful. I hope ya can teach me how to cook like this."

"If'n I can teach the boys to cook a fair meal, I 'spect teachin' you will be a breeze."

John and Maude sat across from them, sipping on tea.

Eva guessed they were waiting to question her and suddenly, she couldn't swallow another bite. But to leave the rest of the food would surely offend Scotty and she forced down the last few forkfuls.

John set his cup down with a click that jarred along Eva's nerves. "Eva, can you tell us a little about yourself?"

"Aye, and what would ya be wantin' to know?" She pressed her lips together and thought about the speaking lessons she'd had on the train. *Make the words in the front of the mouth. Use your lips more. Jut out your chin a bit.* She must speak better English.

"Where are you from? What about your family?" John prodded. At least he asked kindly.

"I'm from Pictou, Nova Scotia. Birthplace of New Scotland." It seemed important they know she was proud of her heritage. "Me—my father was a fisherman."

"Was?" John asked.

"Aye, he drowned at sea a few months back." The words were brittle on her tongue. They said so little of the shock of learning he was dead, the even greater shock of realizing her neighbors blamed her. And still greater shock, the news that she owned nothing. Maybe not even her name.

Maude reached over the table and squeezed Eva's hand. "I'm sorry, child. And what about your mother?"

"She died four years ago. When I was thirteen." There. That answered a question they hadn't asked. Her age.

"Again, I am sorry," Maude said and John echoed her.

"No other family?" Maude's voice was gentle and brought unexpected tightness to Eva's throat.

"None."

"Well then," John said. "You've come to the right place. This will be your home and your family."

Eva lowered her hands to her lap and kept her face down. It was wonderful to be welcomed and she would do everything in her power to prove she was worthy of it.

The conversation turned to other things. Someone knocked on the door and Eva jolted like the knuckles had been put to her chest.

A man stepped in without waiting for an invite.

"Dillon, come in," John called.

Eva saw a man with brown hair and blue eyes. Eyes that stalled when he saw her.

"Saw the wagon and thought Pete would need help unloading it." Still, his gaze stayed on her.

Pete was on his feet. "Eva, this is Dillon that I told you about. Dillon, my wife, Eva."

"What did he tell you about me? Wait a minute, did you say wife?"

"I did."

Eva told herself that Pete seemed pleased with his announcement. But the shock and surprise on Dillon's face informed her that not everyone would be so pleased. Not that she could fault them for that.

"Well, well. Welcome. I hope you don't find this big guy too difficult to live with."

The words dropped into a well of silence. Eva guessed she was the one to empty that well.

"I think we will do just fine."

Dillon grinned. "Guess it's too late to warn you."

"Aye, 'tis."

Dillon chuckled. "All the best." He turned to Pete. "Want a hand unloading the wagon?"

"Sure." Pete grabbed his hat from where he'd hung it. He paused at the doorway. "You'll be okay until I get back."

She wasn't sure it was a question or a statement. "Aye."

But as soon as he stepped out of sight, her heart

knotted something fierce. Every beat sent pain pulsing along her veins.

She was here for one purpose. To be of help. And before anyone could notice she was failing on that score, she pushed to her feet and gathered up the dishes she and Pete had used.

"What do ya think yer doin'?" Scotty asked.

"I'll clean up our mess."

"Not today, little lady. Today yer a guest. Leave it be."

She looked at the older man, saw the firmness yet kindness in his eyes. She shifted her attention to Maude and John.

"Enjoy a few days getting used to the place," Maude said.

"Enjoy getting to know Pete," John added.

Outnumbered and not wanting to make a fuss, she set the dishes back on the table. "Will ya excuse me then?"

"Of course," Maude said.

Eva hurried from the room and up the stairs. She didn't slow down until she reached the bedroom she was to share with Pete. She sank to the edge of the bed, willing her heart to return to its normal rate.

Restless, she circled the room, studying it. She'd seen his clothes in the wardrobe. A smile curved her lips. Wou'nae it be somethin' to see him in that white shirt? Handsome, he'd be, for certain. She paused at the dresser to look at his brush beside hers. A blue checkered neckerchief had been tossed there. She lifted it, pressed it to her nose. It smelled like dust and horses and Pete himself. She chuckled. Good thing no one could read her thoughts and demand an explanation. There was a bit of leather string and a button that must have fallen from something of his. She'd sew it back on as soon as she discovered where it came from.

She continued to circle the room, pausing at the window. To one side, the mountains filled the sky, tossing out pink and orange and purple banners. 'T was a sight to behold. And she let it fill her heart with praise to the Lord above. She shifted her attention to the other side and smiled. Below her, across the trail and behind the cabins, Pete and Dillon unloaded the lumber. They worked quickly, but would that keep them from talking? Keep Dillon from asking questions?

She planted her hands on the window sill and breathed deeply.

Marrying Pete and coming here seemed good in her mind, but she was'nae so naïve as to believe everyone would approve.

Or that they'd learn to live together without encountering stormy seas.

5

Pete grabbed a stack of boards and handed them to Dillon. He moved quickly, intent on keeping the other man so busy there'd be no time for questions.

Dillon took the boards and lowered them to the growing pile. He stood upright and wiped his brow. "Slow down, will you?"

Pete, about to pick up another bundle, stopped and took a deep breath. He wiped his forehead on his shirt sleeve. "We need to get this done and covered with canvas before it gets dark."

"We will. But I know that isn't why you are going at such a furious pace."

"I'm sure you're going to tell me my reasons."

"I sure am. Pete, who is this Eva?"

Pete narrowed his eyes and gave the other man his best don't-mess-with-me look. Apparently, his look had lost its effectiveness, for Dillon ignored the warning.

"She's my wife," he growled.

"Far as I know, you had written to a young lady by the name of Trudy. As I recall, you were going to ask her to come west and meet you with the idea of marriage. Trudy. Not Eva."

"Yup." He had no intention of telling Dillon the details. He lifted boards and shoved them toward Dillon.

"So that's how it's going to be?"

"Yup." Before Dillon could put the load down, Pete had another waiting for him.

Dillon lifted his hands, refusing to take the boards. "You got something you don't want to say?"

"Nope."

"Where did you meet Eva? And when?"

"Here. Take these." Pete shoved the lumber at him.

"Not until you answer my questions?" Dillon crossed his arms and leaned back.

"Maybe I don't think it's any of your business." He kept his voice mild. "In fact, I don't consider it anyone's business but mine and Eva's."

"Huh. One might think you had a secret you don't want us to know about." Dillon studied Pete hard. "That true?"

Pete let out a long-suffering sigh. "At this rate, we are going to be here all night."

Dillon hooted. "And you're anxious to get back to

your bride. I get it." He took the stack from Pete, grinning widely as he straightened. Suddenly his mouth flattened. "Pete, I wish you all the best, but if you're hiding something, you know it will eventually come out."

"That a fact? Then it's a good thing I've nothing to hide." Hiding was different than not spilling private matters.

They finished unloading the wagon and covered the stack of lumber. Dillon accompanied Pete to the barn where they parked the wagon and took care of the horses. Dillon talked about little Neil and what he was doing now. "The boy is smart. You should see how he smiles when he sees me."

They finished and left the barn.

Dillon clapped Pete on the back. "Maybe you'll have a little baby of your own soon."

Pete crossed the yard. There'd be no babies because his arrangement with Eva did not include sleeping together. An arrow pierced his heart. He pretended otherwise. It wasn't like he wanted children. In fact, he hardly ever thought of it. That picture book he'd found on the trail and brought home was only so it wouldn't be ruined. It wasn't because, when he picked it up, he'd thought of saving it for his future children. Even then he knew that would never be.

He thought it was because of his dark skin. But Eva didn't seem to mind that. Or so she said. He couldn't let himself believe things wouldn't change. Nor would he acknowledge that he was afraid to undo the locks on his heart. After all, he wasn't afraid of anything.

He stepped into the house expecting everyone to have retired, but Maude and John sat at the table, the lit lantern in the middle, casting dark shadows on their faces. If he didn't know them better, he might be tempted to think they were cross.

"You got the lumber off all right?" John asked.

"And covered with canvas in case it rains."

"I'm eager to get started on the building." John couldn't help with the construction, but he was more than capable of supervising.

"Weather looks good," Pete said. "We should be able to start tomorrow."

Maude and John looked at each other, some kind of message passing between them.

John spoke. "You can take off a little time to show your wife around. This is all new to her." A beat of expectant waiting.

"She's anxious to help," Pete said.

"Why not spend the rest of the week letting her adjust. Give us all a chance to get to know her."

Pete swallowed hard. John's suggestion was more of an order. It was Wednesday. That gave him three days to spend with Eva. Sunday would see the entire crew assembled, putting an end to time alone with her. Would she welcome the idea of the two of them together or insist she must get to work? It might be wise not to mention the second part of John's order—

to let the others get to know her. That would likely send her running into the woods, never to be found again.

"Very well, if that's what you want." He pushed to his feet. "I'll help John to bed." In the past, one of the boys had always stayed at the house to assist the man. Now that they were all married, that left Pete. Of course, he was married now too, but he was expected to live in the house.

"I won't take long." John rolled into the bedroom across the hall that he shared with Maude. Pete assisted him in preparing for bed then helped him transfer onto the mattress.

"Thank you," John said when he was tucked under the covers. He caught Pete's hand before he stepped away. "I know Eva isn't the young woman you were corresponding with. I don't know what happened with that arrangement, but so long as both you and Eva are happy together, I don't need to know." He patted Pete's hand. "She looks like a lovely young woman."

"Thank you," Pete said, meaning John's understanding as well as his approval of Eva.

John waved him away. "Now go to her."

Maude brought a cup of water for John and bade Pete goodnight. Pete took a pitcher of warm water from the kitchen. As he climbed the stairs, he wondered what awaited him in the bedroom. She would be asleep by now, he reasoned.

He stepped into the room, letting his eyes adjust to the unlit area.

Eva sat on the edge of the bed her fingers intertwined.

"I thought you'd be asleep. Is something wrong?"

"No. I dinna know what you expected."

He put the water down and sat on the edge of his bed, facing her. "I thought we were clear on that matter. You sleep in this bed. I sleep in that one. No expectations of anything else."

"Aye. If yer certain?"

"I agreed and I don't go back on my word." He thought of that little picture book in the dresser. Why was he even keeping it? By rights, he should give it to Neil. But he knew he wouldn't.

She let out a long breath. "I watched you unload lumber, then you disappeared."

"We had to take care of the horses."

She nodded. "I knew that."

"But?"

"I was alone." Her voice quivered.

"I'm here now." He wanted to promise he would always be there, but that wasn't possible. There would be days, weeks even, that he was out with the herd. On those days, one of the other boys would stay behind to assist John, though they would spend the night in their own home.

Maybe John and Maude were right in thinking she

needed a few days with him at her side to help her learn to feel comfortable.

"Aye. I wou'dae washed and prepared for bed but I dinna have water."

"I brought some. Why don't you wash first?"

"Aye." She swallowed audibly. "I 'ave never disrobed and washed in front of a man."

"Tell you what. Why don't we set up one of the other bedrooms as a dressing room?" Without waiting for her answer, he took the water to the room next to his and lit the lamp. She followed, her nightwear clutched to her chest. "I'll leave you," he said. "Take your time."

He returned to the bedroom they were to share and stared out the window. A faint rim of gold edged the mountains. The enormity of what he'd done—married a woman he didn't know—tightened his chest muscles until he could hardly breathe. It had seemed reasonable at the time, but now doubts and fears arose. She'd promised forever, even as he had. But he'd heard such promises before.

"I'm done." Her soft words startled him. He turned. She stood clothed in white, her hair brushed and hanging down her back in a braid. Even in the dim light, he could see how wide her eyes were and how stark her freckles against her skin. She was as uncertain as he and his own fears fled.

"You go to bed. I'll be back in a few minutes." He squeezed her shoulder as he passed, resisting the urge to hold her and assure her everything was going to be fine.

He took his time washing and preparing for bed. Preparing for bed meant only shucking out of his boots, socks, jeans, and shirt. He put out the lamp and tiptoed into the other room.

The lump under the covers informed him Eva was in bed. He couldn't tell if she'd fallen asleep, but just in case, he slid under his quilt as quietly as possible and lay on his back, breathing slowly and silently.

"Good night," she whispered.

"I thought you might be sleeping."

"Och, no. My mind is too busy."

He put his hands beneath his head. "Mine too. What's yours busy with?"

"It might be the rudeness of Mr. Sharp. Or maybe the wedding conducted by a man in a red jacket. Or perhaps the long journey across the grassy hill. Aye, and didn't the grass roll on and on like an ocean? Then again, it might be seeing this grand house. I'm only used to a wee home."

He heard her shift in bed.

"Then again, it might be thinking of meself as a married woman. Aye, all of that is about enough, wou'nae ya say?"

He chuckled softly. "You're saying you're overwhelmed?"

"It's a lot, but if making this arrangement work depends on me, then it will be successful, indeed."

"Because you're a stubborn miss?"

"Determined."

"Me too. Now go to sleep."

"I'll try." Again, her bed covers rustled, but she was quiet.

He lay in the adjacent bed. Tired, but sleep did not come. He shifted, hoping the sound wouldn't disturb her.

"Mama used to read me stories." Her voice came from the darkness. "Or when the lights were out, she'd make them up."

"Tell me one of your stories."

"Aye, and have ya heard of Rob Roy?"

"Afraid not. Is it one of your mother's stories?"

"Aye. One of her favorites. Do ya want to hear it?"

"Please." He got comfortable, ready to enjoy listening to her. "Oh, by the way, before I forget. You and I have the next three days to explore the countryside and get familiar with the place." There, didn't that sound better than the way John had put it?

"Och, but aren't I here to work?"

"You'll get plenty of time for that. Now tell me about Rob Roy."

"Rob Roy MacGregor is his name. He was an ancestor of mine on me mother's side. He was a Scottish hero. Though some might see him as an outlaw. The name MacGregor was banned, but that dinna end the clan. Rob Roy was a tall, handsome man with red hair."

He smiled into the darkness at her emphasis on the words *red hair*.

She continued. "He was a mighty swordsman from his youth. There wasn't a duel he dinna partake of. Ya might be interested to know he was also a cattleman in the highlands. He'd drive cattle south to the lowlands and sell them. He was also a canny businessman and charged others for protection against rustling. Of course, being the man who controlled the rustlers, the arrangement worked very well for him. If certain people weren't agreeable to paying for protection, their herds went missing."

Her voice, round and full, soothed Pete's mind.

She continued. "Aye, but the day came when he borrowed money he cou'nae repay and the Duke of Montrose declared him an outlaw. The Duke's men took over Rob Roy's land and house. They took over his wife too, if ya know what I mean."

He did but couldn't summon the energy to say so.

"'Tis said the poor man died from an infection in a wound suffered in a duel. But his courage and cunning are a matter of pride to all his descendants."

"Hmm."

She chuckled softly. "And I've put ya to sleep. Goodnight, Pete."

He thought he heard her add under her breath, "My husband."

A smile accompanied him to dreamland.

Eva put her palm under her right cheek, smiling into the darkness. Beside her, separated by a few feet, Pete breathed deeply and evenly. The poor man needed his sleep.

Her thoughts shifted to his announcements that they had three days to explore the country. Did that mean just the two of them? If so, it sounded delightful. Meeting the others and trying to make conversation with them made her stomach roll like they were on a trip on her father's boat.

Like she'd said to Pete, she felt safe with him. Not that she could explain that to anyone, including herself. 'T was a good thing there was not anyone who'd be asking for an explanation.

Even if her pa was alive, he wou'nae care. She was but a nuisance to him. Make his meals, wash his dungarees, but other than that, leave him be.

She imagined going exploring with Pete. She couldn't wait to see what wonders she'd see. With her husband. She turned the word over and over in her mind, liking the way it sounded strong and sharing at the same time.

She wakened the next morning to the sound of Pete moving and hurriedly dropped her feet over the side of the bed. Her toes almost touched his. She raised her eyes slowly. He wore a white union suit. She swallowed hard. And forced her gaze upward. His eyes were dark. Bottomless. Full of an emotion she couldn't identify, but it made her mouth go dry.

"Morning," he said. His husky voice rippled along the surface of her skin.

She managed to choke out something that sounded vaguely like, "Morning."

He yawned and stretched his arms overhead, making her very aware of the breadth of his chest. Like a young stevedore, she thought. All brawn, her pa had said. He'd also added, and no brain, but she knew that didn't apply to Pete.

"Do you want to use the dressing room first?" he asked.

She couldn't pull a word from her brain nor make a muscle of her body move. Not wanting him to think she'd grown daft, she shook her head. "I'll wait."

"Very well." He tromped past on bare feet.

Not until the door closed behind him did her breath reach into her lungs. Realizing she had only a few minutes, she jerked off her nightgown and slipped into a roomy dark gray skirt. Remembering his comment about her flowered dress, she chose a blue shirtwaist dotted with dark blue flowers. She was dressed and mostly in her right mind when he returned, his wavy black hair slicked back, his face gleaming from being washed. He wore jeans—manly, she thought. And a dark gray shirt. Practical. His boots thudded on the floor.

Aye, he was a bonnie man to look at. Dark enough to speak of courage.

"Your turn," he said.

She jolted into action and hurried to the next room to wash.

Finished, she stepped into the hall where he waited.

"I smell coffee." He sounded like he couldn't wait to get a cupful of the stuff.

He was a coffee drinker. She'd keep that in mind. She was more of a tea drinker, as were most of the people she knew back east.

She tucked her hand into the crook of his elbow and walked down the stairs with him. And dinna she cling to his arm as they entered the kitchen.

"Morning, missy. Pete." Scotty set two cups of coffee on the table.

Pete took a drag of one. "I have to help John. I'll be back in a few minutes." He held a chair for Eva, drew a cup of coffee before her, then strode across the hall.

She made out the murmur of voices. The coffee smelled inviting and she took a sip. Blah. It was bitter. She forced the mouthful down but returned the cup to the table and stared at it. Why did anyone drink something like that?

"Not a coffee drinker?"

She should have known Scotty watched. "I dinna think so."

"Tea then, miss?"

"Och, dinna bother about me."

"Tea is no bother." He shook the kettle on the stove, moved it forward to a hotter spot, then went to the tall cupboard and searched for something. In a minute, he brought out a brown-betty teapot, rinsed it with hot water and dumped in a handful of tea leaves. He poured boiling water into the pot and set it and a clean cup in front of her.

Every passing second sent tension up her limbs. She was here to help and instead she was creating more work.

"Thank you," she managed to say. "But please, in the future, I dinna expect to be waited on."

"Missy, I don't mind. It's me job and all."

"Aye, and didn't I understand my job is to help ya?"

Scotty squinted at her. "I'll allow ya to help, but I think yer job is to please that man of yers." He turned back to the stove, hopefully before he saw the color heating her cheeks.

The aroma of frying pork, potatoes, and eggs filled Eva's nostrils.

Maude stepped from the room across the hall, John wheeling after her and Pete in their wake.

Eva's gaze went to that man of hers, as Scotty said. Drawn like it was pulled by a rope. He smiled, sending a delightful tremor through her. She lowered her gaze to the cup in front of her before anyone could take note of her reaction. She knew from the heat in her face that she was a bright red.

Tea. Now, wou'nae that be good about now? She forced her hand not to tremble as she poured herself a cupful.

John sat at one end of the table with Maude across the corner from him, facing Eva as Scotty put out plates and silverware for the meal.

Pete pulled out the chair next to her and sat down. With him beside her, she began to relax and was able to return John and Maude's greetings without stumbling on her words.

Scotty carried the food to the table, then sat at the end.

Something about him joining them eased a tension she hadn't been aware of. It signified he was more friend and less servant. Aye, she liked that.

"I'll ask the blessing." John bowed his head. "Father in heaven, giver of every good gift. We thank You and praise You for the evidence of Your abiding love. Bless this food, bless Eva and Pete as they enjoy each other today. Amen."

As the food was passed from hand to hand, John spoke. "Did Pete tell you he is to show you around the ranch for the next few days? No work for you yet."

"Aye, he did mention it. And I thank ya for yer generosity." She reminded herself of how to form her words correctly and thought she'd done a fair-to-middlin' job.

"It's my pleasure." He turned to Pete. "What do you plan to do today?"

"That depends. Eva, can you ride horseback?"

She'd only done so a handful of times. Mostly she walked or rode in a wagon. But if riding a horse meant doing things with Pete, she was prepared to be an expert on the spot. "I have ridden."

"Good. Then we'll go south. I can show her more of the country. Scotty, can I take food for a noon meal?"

"For the missy, I will pack it myself."

"You dinna need to bother."

"It's no bother. I had about given up hope for Pete, here. To have him bring home a pretty young thing..." Scotty rubbed at his nose. "It's more'n I thought possible."

"Huh?" Pete protested. "You think no one would have me, is that it?"

Scotty shook his head. "More like I thought ya'd chase away every unmarried woman with your scowls and the way you knot yer forehead."

Eva looked from Scotty to Pete. Saw in Pete's eyes a barely concealed wound. Perhaps not from Scotty's words, but from the truth in them. She smiled gently. "I've not seen any scowls. Nothing but smiles, in fact."

Scotty slapped his knees. "Pete, you got yerself a good un with Eva."

John and Maude both agreed.

It warmed the cockles of Eva's heart to hear their words, but what lit a fire within was the pleasure she saw in Pete's eyes.

They finished eating. John reached for a Bible. "It's our habit to read a bit of scripture every morning."

"'Tis a pleasant way to start a day," she said.

"I think so." John opened his Bible. "I am going to read only one verse this morning from John chapter thirteen. 'A new commandment I give unto you, That ye love one another; as I have loved you, that ye also love one another.'" His gaze went from Pete to Eva. "What greater way to start a marriage than to promise to love like Jesus did?"

Eva nodded. She dinna think she could be like Jesus in any way, but it was a noble idea.

Scotty waved away her offer to help.

"Come with me," Pete said.

They were halfway to the door when it opened and Dillon entered, accompanied by a woman and a babe in arms.

"I brought my wife to meet you," Dillon said. "Eva, this is Abby, and my son, Neil." He drew forward a brown-haired woman with brown eyes. And a sweet little bairn who held his arms out to John. John took the wee one, and the two grinned at each other.

"Welcome." Abby's smile was warm.

"Thank you," Eva murmured, watching Abby for her reaction. Bad enough, none of them had ever heard of Eva before. But she must also be shocked at Eva's red hair. Like fire in the woodshed, someone had once said. Not that she'd been the only redhead around. But for some reason, she was the one to be branded for it. She'd never known why until her father drowned.

"We won't stay," Abby said. "But I know what it's like to be new here and feeling a little lost and overwhelmed. Remember we've all been in that situation. You'll find everyone here is kind. If you want a friend, I hope you'll consider me. And the others here. My door is always open. That's all I wanted to say." She reached for her baby.

Pete, with Eva on his arm, followed them outside. "Dillon, Eva and I are going away for the day. Can you see that John has what he needs?"

"Of course. Where are you going?"

Pete pulled Eva closer. "South. Lots to see that direction."

"Lots to see in every direction," Dillon said.

"We have three days to see it," Pete explained how they were given the next three days to explore.

"Be sure and show her the cave, the hoodoos, the—"

Pete held up a hand to stop him. "I think I can figure it out."

Dillon laughed and clapped him on the back. "No doubt. Have a good day." He nodded goodbye to Eva.

"Enjoy yourselves," Abby said.

The pair went toward their cabin and Pete aimed Eva toward the barn. He caught two horses and led them in.

"Do you ride astride or sidesaddle?" he asked.

She considered her answer. Would he be shocked if she said astride? But it was the only way she'd ever ridden. And without a saddle. Perhaps she wou'nae give him details about her riding experience. "Astride is fine."

He brought forward a black horse. "Your horse is called Lady and she's all that. The gentlest sweetest horse ever." Pete put on a saddle blanket and saddle as he talked.

She watched closely, determined she'd learn to do things for herself.

Then he turned to the other horse. Also black but larger than Lady. "This is my horse, Blackie."

"Blackie? And are ya trying to tell people something?"

He left off saddling his horse to look at her. "What do you mean?"

"Seems to me ya worry overmuch about the color of yer skin. Seems to me yer wanting to let everyone know you are aware of it by calling yer horse Blackie. Why not Thunder. Or Smoke?"

"Because there's no point in pretending he's anything but black." He returned to his task.

"Aye. I understand."

He adjusted the saddle then faced her. "What's to understand?"

She smiled, seeing the tender yearning that filled his eyes. "Is he a good horse?"

"The best." Pete patted the animal and rubbed his neck.

"So being black doesn't make him less. Might even make him better."

Pete's hands stilled. He stared at Blackie's neck. Slowly, Pete's gaze came to hers and went deep, searching, probing, exploring. She waited, holding her thoughts still, hoping he would find what he wanted. She knew the minute he did. The skin around his eyes crinkled. Then his mouth twitched. He laughed low in his throat.

"You're saying—"

"Could be that black is better. No matter what shade of the color." Pete was far from black like she'd seen on the docks back in Pictou. Her first impression had been bronze and she hadn't changed her mind.

He handed Lady's reins to her. "Let's go see what Scotty has for our lunch."

They crossed the yard. Scotty stood on the veranda, holding a sack Eva thought might hold enough to last them the entire three days.

"Enjoy yerselves," he said.

Pete hung the sack from his saddle then turned to help Eva to the back of her horse. She pulled her skirt around her legs, glad she'd worn one with lots of fabric. She shifted in the saddle, seeking the best position while Pete adjusted the stirrups to fit her.

Satisfied, he swung into his own saddle. Her horse followed Blackie and Pete from the yard.

Once out of sight, he stopped and studied her. "How much have you ridden before?"

"A few times."

"Can you be more specific?"

"Half a dozen."

His eyes narrowed. "For how long?"

She laughed. "Until I was caught." Seeing his confusion, she continued. "One of the neighbors kept a horse in the pasture behind their house. Sometimes, I would catch him—he could be bribed with carrots—and ride him bareback. Until the mister saw me and ordered me to go home." Her voice dropped. "Called me a bad name. Said I was the spawn of Satan."

Pete urged his horse closer. "People really said those kinds of things to you?"

"Aye." She lowered her gaze to hide the tears rushing up.

"I don't think I like Easterners if that's what they're like."

She brought her gaze back to his. "Och, but haven't you had unkind things said about you?"

"Some, but mostly I've been dismissed as if I had no more value than a dog. But that's different."

"How?"

His eyes held hers in a steady gaze that offered

something she cou'nae remember having before. Nor could she find a name for it.

"Because you should be protected."

She wanted to laugh, dismiss the idea, and say she didn't need protection. But she cou'nae. It felt that good to think someone cared enough about her to want to protect her.

But dare she believe Pete wou'nae change his mind once he knew her better? And if he should ever learn the awful truth she'd only recently discovered, he would react the same way her neighbors had.

6

Pete waited to see how Eva would respond to him saying he wanted to protect her. Would she laugh at the idea? Be dismissive? Or would she welcome it?

"Aye, maybe neither of us deserves the unkind things that are said and done."

"I agree." More for her than for him. The losses and rejections he'd felt were but distant memories. Having found a home and acceptance at the ranch had erased the pain from his past. More or less. "Now let me give you a few riding lessons so you can enjoy this day. First—" He told her how to hold the reins, how to guide the horse, and how to sit in her saddle and use her legs to keep from bouncing.

She was a quick learner, eager to follow his suggestions. She laughed at her mistakes and was easily distracted by the clouds floating by, the color of the grass, and a hundred things, but her attention returned to him as quickly as it left.

He would have been half content to stay where they were and talk, but if they meant to see the sights, he wanted to show her they must move on.

"Are you ready to ride now?" he asked.

She laughed, amusement making sparkles dance in her eyes. "Aye, and wasn't I ready before you showed me how to ride?"

"You wouldn't have suffered in silence, wouldn't you?"

"Aye." She ducked her head, but not before he'd seen pink flooding her cheeks.

"Are you that stubborn?" His tone was gentle, interested rather than judgmental.

"No, 'tis determined, I am." Her head slowly came up. Pink still filled her cheeks. But her eyes were steady, serious. "I am determined to explore the countryside with you." Pink turned to red in her face.

She wanted to be with him that badly? He swallowed hard. Tried to find a word or two to say. His mind was completely and totally blank, his thoughts swallowed up by surprise and gladness at the idea.

"Then let's go explore." The words choked from his tight throat.

They rode side by side, taking their time. After all, they had no place to be, nothing to do but enjoy the sunshine and their time together.

As he'd told Dillon and John he would, he rode south, pointing out every detail of the scene.

"More wildflowers. In June, you'll get to see and smell wild roses growing along the edge of the trees. The scent fills the air."

Eva looked at the trees, then brought her gaze to him. "I cannae wait to smell them."

He forgot about the wild roses at the glow in her cheeks. "You're much like a bright red rose yourself." Now why had he blurted that aloud? Would she be terribly offended?

But to his surprise, she laughed, low and gentle. "Aye, I've been called many a thing but never a red rose." Her eyes brimmed with amusement and something more. He couldn't put a name to it, but it made him feel rather pleased with himself and he chuckled as they rode onward.

"Earlier in the season, we see baby hawks in that nest." He pointed to the tree. "This summer, a doe and twin fawns were often seen in this area." Hoping they might see the trio, he signaled for them to stop. But nothing moved and after a few minutes, they continued.

He turned to the west. They passed by the remains of a campsite.

"Who would have made that?" she asked.

"Travelers. Usually, men headed west in search of gold."

"Gold, ya say? It's found nearby?"

Recalling the words that were branded in his brain, he said, "Don't be fool enough to fall for false hope."

She laughed softly again. It was like the sound of distant water tumbling over polished rocks. "I'd never be the one to leave something sure to go after a possibility."

"Me either." Did she mean him as something sure? He'd certainly do his best to live up to that assessment.

They rode further until a huge boulder came into view. Surrounded by rolling grassland, the rock had a furrow around it.

"Do you know what this is?" he asked, guessing she wouldn't. He certainly hadn't until it had been pointed out to him.

"A wee bit of a rock?" She spoke with such innocence that he almost believed she meant it. Then her eyes flashed and he knew she was joshing him.

He laughed. "When we go into the mountains and see the rock cliffs, it really does suddenly appear to be small. Come and have a closer look." He dismounted and lifted her down. She grimaced as her legs took her weight but then she smiled, refusing to admit she felt any discomfort from being in the saddle all morning.

He took her hand as if she needed guiding toward the 'wee rock' even though he knew she didn't.

She touched it, ran her fingers along the polished spots.

"It's a buffalo rub," he said. "Every time the bison pass this spot they scratch themselves on the rock.

Their rough coats have worn the rock to a glassy finish there and there." He pointed, but she had already found the smooth places.

"Have ya seen them for yerself?"

"Afraid not. There were very few left by the time I got here. But there used to be thousands of them roaming the plains. I've heard stories of great brown masses thundering over the hills."

She looked into the distance. "'Twould have been a sight to behold. What happened to them?"

"They were hunted. Some say for their hides. Some say as bait for catching wolves. Some say because they caused problems with the trains."

Her gaze bored into him. "Are ya saying ya don't think those to be the reason?"

"I think they had something to do with it, but I wonder if the whites didn't kill as many as they could to starve the Indians."

Her mouth fell open. Shock darkened her eyes. She blinked. "Och, no."

They wandered around the rock as they talked. Having circled it, he drew her up to the level ground, caught the reins of the horses, and led them to a nearby grove of trees. "Let's eat here while I tell you about this place."

They sat side by side, looking toward the rock, and onward to the rolling hills to the east and the mountains to the west. He opened the sack and drew out the food Scotty had prepared. Chuckled when he saw Scotty had included items he reserved for a special occasion—cookies from his secret store, pieces of cheese—where did Scotty hide that?—and a can of peaches. There were thick sandwiches made with Scotty's good bread and filled with slices of meat and his special mustard sauce. Carrots from the garden washed until their outer skin had been removed.

He asked the blessing, so grateful, not only for the food but for the company. He took a few bites of his sandwich before Eva nudged him. "Did ya forget something?"

He knew what she meant but pretended ignorance. "Have I?"

"Och, yer a teasing man. Ya did say you would tell me more about this place."

"Of course. Are you sure you want to hear?"

She jabbed her fists to her hips and glowered at him. "Tell me." The look lasted about a second before she burst out laughing.

He laughed too, then settled back against a tree. "This is one of my favorite places on the ranch." He slanted a look at her. "You're wondering why, aren't you?"

She nodded. "Aye."

"I had visited the rub often. John had told us what it was and I was fascinated to think of herds of those huge beasts topping that hill, grazing the green grass and stopping to scratch themselves here. I came out here when I wanted to be alone. I guess it's kind of my place."

"Have I invaded yer alone place?"

He caught her hand. "I brought you because I wanted to share it with you."

Pink colored her face.

He touched her cheek. "Have I embarrassed you? Made you uncomfortable?"

"Och, no. 'Tis pleased, I am, that ya think to show me things that matter to ya."

Their gazes held unblinkingly. In that moment something sealed between them. At least in his mind. He wanted her to be a part of every corner of his life.

The acknowledgment burned through his thoughts. And settled like a restless beast inside his chest. The bit of paper on which their names were linked in marriage provided the promise of forever, but he knew the folly of thinking it meant their hearts would unite. He gave a little cough and shifted his attention to the rock.

"One time, I met a native man here with his son. The man said he wanted to teach his boy how things used to be. When there was plenty of good hunting and they were free to roam along the mountains. He said his son had never seen a buffalo herd. Wondered how he could be a true Piikani without the knowing how to bring down a buffalo."

Eva shifted her attention from the rock to Pete and never looked away again as he continued his story.

"It was only a few years since his tribe had signed a treaty. The man I met said the mighty warriors believed they were negotiating for peace, not a land settlement. I'll never forget how he hung his head, his hands limp at his side as he said, 'We are no longer a proud people.'"

"Och, this a sad story. Did ya ever see them again?"

"No, the pair rode away. I watched until they were out of sight. But when I hear people in town saying unkind things about the natives, I remember the way that man sounded."

"Do ya correct them?"

He shrugged. "Most people don't want to have their opinions challenged. Nor would they change their mind if I told them they were wrong." He opened the can of peaches and speared out a half for her. She took it and nibbled it as if delighting in each taste. He watched without taking a half for himself.

She lifted her eyes to him. "Am I doing something wrong?"

"Just never saw anyone eat a peach like that."

Her eyebrows quirked. "How do ya eat a peach?"

For an answer, he speared out a half and popped it into his mouth whole.

"Aye, I like to enjoy every bite."

He chewed and swallowed. Wiped his mouth. "Me too." He waited, wondering how she'd respond.

"The difference is, I enjoy a dozen bites to yer one."

He grinned. Her assessment was so unexpected

and so accurate. "And I get to enjoy the view." He kept his gaze on her, not the scene before them, wondering if she would understand that he meant her.

Then she widened her eyes and held his gaze, not even flinching when her cheeks flushed. Something flickered in her irises, creased the skin at the edges of her eyes and pulled at the corners of her mouth. "Aye, I do too."

It was all he could do not to jerk back in surprise. She liked what she saw?

She grinned at him. "Any more peaches left?"

He gave her another half and took the last half for himself. She nibbled at hers and he ate his whole and their eyes said things that surprised him. And likely her too. Not that he could name what he saw. Respect. Affection. Enjoyment. All that and more?

The peaches were gone. They ate cookies and sat in companionable stillness, listening to the birds overhead, the buzz of insects, and the *kee-eeeee-arr* of a hawk soaring so far overhead it was but a dot.

The food was gone. Eva put the remains of their lunch back in the sack but apart from that, neither of them moved. He couldn't speak for her feelings, but it felt good just to be at her side.

He detected a movement in the grass nearby and touched her hand, signaling her to be quiet. A rabbit sat up on its hindquarters, its nose twitching and its ears perked up as it studied its surroundings.

Both Eva and Pete sat motionless until the rabbit hopped away.

She laughed softly. "Now all we need is to see a tortoise."

He knew the story of the tortoise and the hare. "We were told that story in the orphanage in the hopes of encouraging us to never give up on a difficult task."

"Such as?"

"Can you milk a cow?"

"No. Will I be expected to?"

"I don't think so, but it's one of the things I had to learn. I was afraid of the man in the barn who was to teach me. He didn't mind using the toe of his boot to instruct, if you know what I mean?"

She pressed her hand to his forearm. "Aye, I do. And I dinna like it. If I had a child, I would be patient no matter what." She lowered her gaze and withdrew her hand. "Och, but I'll not have a child."

He felt the pain of her acknowledgment in the pit of his stomach. He wanted to say things could change, their agreement could be altered, but he'd given his word and if a man can't keep his promises, he was less than a man.

Rather than letting her wallow in lost possibilities, he got to his feet, held out a hand to help her up. She took his hand and gained her feet. She stood before him, looking into his eyes.

"I dinna mean I have any regrets. I agreed, knowing

full well what I agreed to. I will be faithful to my word."

He nodded. It was what he wanted. Wasn't it? Nothing more.

EVA RODE beside Pete as they resumed exploring the countryside. 'T was amazing to see the vast rolling land. She shou'nae mentioned children. Their agreement made such impossible. She wou'nae mourn the idea. Hoping to put an end to the uneasiness between them that was her fault she said, "'Tis like an ocean of grass."

"I've never seen the ocean, so I'll have to take your word for it."

"The ocean is a restless beast. One minute 'tis calm and gentle, the next, a raging, roaring bit of anger."

"Don't be mistaken. The weather out here can also change abruptly and turn nasty." He looked around at the horizon on every side. "It's wise to keep an eye on the sky." He pointed to the west. "The worst storms come over the mountains. If you see thunder clouds building that direction, head for shelter."

"It looks like a person would get plenty of warnin'."

"Sometimes. But a person should be careful all the same." He turned in his saddle. "Promise me you'll be careful when you're by yourself."

"Aye, of course." It was an easy promise to give. She

would have liked to beg the same promise from him, but dinna she suspect that his life as a cowboy might involve his taking risks that would frighten her? If'n she saw the cows and watched him at work, would it relieve her worries or increase them? There was so much she didn't know about her husband—her tongue lingered on that word—and life on a ranch. Och, but didn't she have time to learn it?

"Where are we goin' now?" she asked.

"No place special." He chuckled. "Though that isn't exactly true. There are special things everywhere. But I thought you might like to venture into the mountains a bit."

"Aye, I would." Nor would she utter one word about the way her legs grumbled about riding.

They rode side by side, steadily climbing, circling around rocky outcrops and passing by more and more trees. Many of the leaves were yellow or gold. She inhaled the scent of fall.

They reached a viewpoint. He reined in, helped her down, and then guided her forward. She gasped. Below them lay a valley filled with a mixture of evergreen trees and deciduous ones. The latter were a golden yellow—almost orange. "'Tis a sight to behold. The trees back home turn red and gold but I've never seen a valley of trees, wearing their colors like ribbons on a full skirt."

He held her hand and let her take in her fill.

She sighed long, releasing her breath slowly for fear she might blow away the scene.

He sat on the grassy slope and pulled her down to sit beside him. To his credit, he dinna seem inclined to talk as she simply drank in the view, letting the peace and beauty of it settle into her heart.

"Aye, 'tis a good thing Mr. Sharp turned down my offer of marriage." Never mind that it had been his offer that brought her out expecting to gain a husband. Which she had done. Just not the one she thought to have.

He squeezed her hand. "I'd say his loss is my gain."

"And mine." She believed she'd found a good man. In the few hours she'd known him, she felt safer with him than she had ever before, even with her own pa. "I believe ya will treat me kindly."

"Of course I will." He leaned back on his elbows and studied her. "Did you not have a happy home?"

"Mostly, I'd say I did. Until Mama died. Then my father dinna care much for me company. So long as I made his tea, put food on the table, and kept him in clean trousers, he dinna want anything more." She'd never before admitted how much it hurt to have her father treat her like she was invisible.

"It sounds like you had a lonely life. For some reason, it seems your neighbors treated you poorly and your father didn't want your company."

The skin around her eyes tightened and she knew

he'd be reading her agreement even without her uttering a word.

He sat up and took her hands between his. "We have both known unkindness and rejection. Our life together need never know that." His thumbs rubbed the back of her hands. His smile contained both promise and longing. "Like you said, we can forget the past and look only to the future."

His dark bottomless eyes invited her to accept and partake of his offer. She was only too glad to do so.

"Aye, I believe we can do that."

A large bird swooped past them. She felt the wind of its wide wings, heard the air sift through its feathers. It dove into the tree tops far below. The branches bounced and shifted and then all was calm.

"Was'nae that something. A bird that close."

"It was a golden eagle," he said matter-of-factly.

"An eagle, ya say. 'Tis a good omen."

"What do you mean by an omen?"

"'Tis said that an eagle is a sign that good things lie in the future." She laughed. Cou'nae contain her joy, bounced to her feet, and twirled in a circle. "I remember something my ma would say on a particularly good day. 'The lines are fallen unto me in pleasant places.'" Eva looked down into Pete's amused face. "'Tis from the Good Book ya know."

"Pleasant places, you say?"

"I do indeed." She pointed upward. "Look at the vast sky. The beauty of the trees, the mighty mountains." She lowered her finger to indicate what she meant. Her hand fell to her side. "And a husband." Someone who'd promised to love and honor. She could do with a fair bit of both.

She fell into his gaze, mesmerized, floating.

He rose slowly, his eyes never leaving hers. He stood before her, dark eyes guarded.

Had she said too much? Aye, and she had never been one to keep her thoughts to herself. But for the first time, she could recall she was prepared to keep her words locked up inside if they offended Pete.

She waited as he faced her. Preparing her mind to apologize and hide her feelings if he was offended by her frankness.

7

Pete studied the woman before him. His wife. Strange thought. But at least it provided some assurance that she would stay.

She was unlike any other woman he'd encountered. Speaking emotions freely. Enjoying life with abandon. Like a butterfly flitting from flower to flower to drink sweet nectar. She made his world seem sweeter.

The spark in her eyes had dampened and she watched him. If he read her expression correctly she was waiting nervously. For what?

Then it hit him. She wanted his approval. He stood taller knowing that what he thought mattered to her. He caught her fingers.

"It's nice we are husband and wife."

Her eyes brightened. Her cheeks grew pinker. His eyes narrowed. "Are you getting sunburned?" She'd worn a hat Maude gave her for most of the day, but it had fallen to her back as they looked out at the valley.

"Am I?" She touched her cheeks. "Aye." She pulled her hat back to her head and tipped it down to provide shade. "'Tis the curse of being a redhead."

He touched her cheek, noting how the heat of the sun had pooled there. "Or perhaps it's one of the blessings."

Her eyes widened. She lifted her hand to his cheek. "I would change my fair skin for your dark. Ya dinna worry about being burned to a crisp."

He caught her hand where it lay against his cheek and held it there. His hand on her face, hers on his. Something stirred in his heart. A distant, forgotten feeling.

Below them, the eagle that had flown so close lifted from the tree tops and sailed away to the west. She believed it meant good things lay in their future. He was quite willing to believe it too.

The sun shone in his eyes. He blinked. "It's getting late. We need to get back for supper." Though if they had enough food, he'd have been happy staying there until sunset. But riding home after dark presented risks he wasn't prepared to take.

Eva's gaze shifted back to the valley below. "I could stay here forever."

Pleased that she expressed such an opinion and hoping he might have a role in her wishes, he chuckled. "You'd soon be wanting a warm and comfortable bed."

She shook her head. "Just a blanket to roll up in 'twould be enough for me." Her gaze returned to him. "Aye, and someone to keep me company."

Knowing she meant him, he couldn't help but smile. He would suggest they return tomorrow with supplies to stay overnight, but there were other places he wanted her to see.

They returned to the horses. He cupped his hands together and indicated she should use them to step up into the saddle. She did so. He patted her leg. It was strange to think that, as her husband, he had the right to touch her.

He turned away and mounted his own horse.

They made their way down the mountain. Sometimes he led the way and other times they rode side by side. For a time, neither of them spoke. No doubt she was tired and he watched her. If he thought she struggled to stay awake, he would take a break.

She released a sigh that stirred the hair in Lady's mane.

"Are you tired?" he asked.

"No. Just thinking."

"Sounded like a heavy thought."

"Aye. Pete, do ya wonder why I thought of marrying Mr. Sharp?"

He hadn't, but now he did. "I can't see you being happy living in town."

"Nor would I. I was so desperate that I was willing to marry the first man that offered. I wanted to leave Pictou and all its memories."

"It's hard losing both parents." And from what she'd said, her neighbors weren't kind to her. "What was it about Mr. Sharp that made you think a marriage to him would be suitable?"

She grew thoughtful. Shook her head. "Mostly that he lived so far west that I was sure I could outrun my memories."

"Don't memories stay with us? Even when we don't welcome them?"

"Aye, but I reasoned if I dinna have to see people and places that constantly reminded me of the things I didn't want to be reminded of, I could start anew." She drew in a sharp breath. "Mr. Sharp said I would have a nice house. He said he could afford to give me all the things I needed. He said he was a regular church goer and an upright citizen." A mirthless chuckle punctuated her statements. "He seemed the right age. Said he was a fair-looking man." She jerked about to stare at Pete. "Dinna he seem pasty-faced though?"

Pete blinked, nodded, and then grinned. "Compared to me that would apply to a lot of men."

She tipped her head back and laughed. She sobered and looked hard into his eyes. "Pasty faced."

She was saying she liked his dark looks? He felt her approval clear through to his bones.

"I dinna ask him the important questions."

"And what would they be?"

"Was he kind? Accepting? Would he let me roam free or insist I be a housebound wife? Things like that."

"I wouldn't expect you to remain in the house."

"Aye and don't I know it? Riding with you is better than wandering alone. Will we do it often?"

He laughed. Not in amusement, but in pleasure to know she wanted his company. "We will do it very often." The future looked brighter than ever before. They would soon be back at the ranch in time for supper, but he wished he could stretch the day out another eight hours or more. Back at the ranch, they would be met by curious, inquisitive people. All very kindly, but he liked having Eva to himself.

They took a break at the buffalo rub rock. He helped her down. It took a few seconds for her to stand straight when her feet hit the ground. He couldn't help but notice she moved stiffly, but she didn't complain.

"Will we see any natives, do ya think?" she asked.

"Occasionally a few will ride by. Some know John and Maude and stop to visit, but mostly they stay on the land they agreed to take, their spirits heavy." Now, why had he made it sound like he knew how they felt? He sympathized because he understood what it felt like to see dreams taken away, but he couldn't say how the natives felt. Except for the man he'd seen at the Buffalo rub.

"Och, I hope they come to visit so I can see them for meself."

"You aren't afraid?"

"Are they not friendly?"

"For the most part. Though there have been objectors. A couple years ago, there was a rebellion north of here. Quite a ways north," he added when he saw her concern. "The leader and some of his followers were hanged."

She shuddered, so he hurried on.

"A civilian militia was formed under the control of the North West Mounted Police. Maude sent me and Dillon to join them. I'm grateful to say we never had to take part in any battle, but for a few weeks we rode back and forth on the border with Montana. Mostly we turned back any natives who thought to join the rebellion. And then it was over and we went back home."

"It sounds exciting and scary all at once."

He shrugged. "Some excitements we can do without."

"Aye, that's God's truth."

He gave her a questioning look.

She grinned. "It's something my ma would say from time to time." She got a faraway look in her eyes. "I have not thought of her as much as I should. Wou'nae she be disappointed in me?"

Pete touched her shoulder, drawing her attention to him. "Eva, I think she would be proud of the strong young woman you are." If she wouldn't have been, she was not a fit mother, but he wouldn't say that to Eva. It would be hurtful.

"Strong? Aye? How so?"

"No shrinking violet would undertake a journey across Canada with plans to marry a man she'd never met."

Her eyes reflected the late afternoon sun, bright and clear. "Aye, and haven't you said I am a blooming rose?"

"And I haven't changed my mind."

They resumed their homeward journey, taking their time. Stopping often to watch a bird, study the leaves on a tree that were dancing like golden coins—her words, not his—and talking about things.

"Have ya ever wanted to have a place of yer own?"

"No," he said. "Maude and John have given me a family. I will take care of them out of gratitude."

"Only gratitude?" She watched him closely.

His first reaction was to close off his expression, perhaps even his heart, to admitting any more, but her openness with her emotions convinced him that she would expect the same from him. He had no wish to disappoint her. "Out of gratitude and love." The last word felt awkward on his tongue and he realized it was the first time he'd ever spoken it.

"'Tis good to hear."

He didn't ask if she meant it was good to hear of

his affection for the older couple or to hear the word love from his lips.

At least she wouldn't be expecting him to say the word to her. Which was a good thing. He was not willing to take a risk on opening his heart to that pain.

THE RANCH BUILDINGS came into sight.

Eva would be glad to stop riding, but she dinna want to end the day with Pete. He was an excellent guide, full of interesting stories. All of which revealed his kind, loyal nature.

If only she and Pete could be on their own. John, Maude, and Scotty seemed like good people. Dillon too. She guessed the others would be nice enough. But she'd learned people could be nice to your face while harboring dark feelings and secrets.

Was there something she could do to delay their return? She looked around in search of a distraction. Aye, some bright flowers to one side. She could ask to pick a bouquet. Or see what was behind that hill. Or look at the big rock nearby. But that would be purely selfish. Pete needed to get back and these people were his friends and family. For his sake, she would smile and make conversation with them. To the best of her ability.

She didn't speak a single word of complaint or reluctance as they rode closer and closer.

They went directly to the barn. She wanted to be strong and manage on her own but discovered her body to be less willing. He lifted her from the saddle and lowered her to the ground. Her legs protested. Pete must have suspected her problem for he held her as she forced her limbs to do their job.

Not that she minded his hands on her arms or the excuse to lean into them. In fact, it felt nice. How long had it been since she'd felt a warm touch? An embrace? A word of love? Since Mama died. Of course, she knew her arrangement with Pete allowed no room for love but still, his arms felt nice and strong.

Her legs held her but she didn't immediately straighten. Just a few more minutes of enjoyin' being held. That's all she wanted. Only her heart told her a few minutes wou'nae be enough. Never.

Knowing that, she forced herself to edge back. "Thank ya."

"For what?" One hand lingered on her upper arm. Was he as reluctant to end his hold as she was to leave it?

"For the adventure of this day. For telling me so many things."

His eyebrows went up in a silent question.

"About the buffalo, the Indians, the roses—" She felt heat in her cheeks at the mention of roses.

He grinned. Obviously remembering his words on the subject. A red rose. She liked that idea.

She continued. "For taking me riding and being patient with me."

He moved his hand up and down her arm in warm caresses. "It was entirely my pleasure."

"Not entirely. 'Twas mine too."

A sound outside the barn ended the tender moment. He lowered his hand. She stepped back.

A half-grown boy stepped into the barn and skidded to a halt. Blond hair poked out from under a cap. Blue eyes darted from Pete to Eva and stalled there.

"Hi, Boyd. Everything all right?" Pete asked.

The boy swallowed audibly. "Yeah. Lainie sent me to get some oats for the chickens." He swallowed loudly again.

"Boyd, this my wife, Eva."

The boy formed the word wife silently.

Pete continued. "Eva, this is Boyd. Remember I told you about Noah and Lainie? He's Lainie's brother."

"Pleased to meet ya," Eva said.

"Hi."

Pete shifted his attention back to Boyd. "Are Lainie and Missy all right?"

Boyd nodded vigorously. "Lainie's making supper." Those words jolted him into action. "I better get back." He ran out the door.

"Don't forget the oats," Pete called.

The boy skidded to a halt and returned. He grabbed a bucket, marched to the end of the barn, dipped the bucket into a cupboard, and hurried back out with it full of oats. Calling goodbye, he trotted away.

Pete chuckled. "Guess we surprised him some."

"Dinna like being a surprise." She tried but failed to keep a sharp note from her voice.

Pete draped an arm across her shoulders. "Eva, you are a good surprise and don't you forget it."

She ducked her head, startled at his words. Then smiled up at him, her eyes sheltered by her lashes.

To the best of her ability, she helped him unsaddle and take care of the horses. He instructed her gently. A couple times as she brushed Lady, he covered her hand to show her what to do.

Or was it an excuse to touch her? A little burst of sweetness exploded in her heart to think so.

All too soon for her peace of mind, the horses were tended and they walked to the house. From the veranda, John and Maude watched them approach. Her steps slowed so much that Pete stopped and turned toward her.

"Eva? Something wrong?"

"Och, no. Nothing apart from me red hair and freckles and face that is likely to be glowing like tomorrow's sunrise. Apart from strangers wanting to know more about me than I be wanting to tell. Apart from feeling like I am a new arrival in an unfamiliar land. No, nothing at all."

He laughed. "I think there is a verse in the Good

Book. 'Be not forgetful to entertain strangers: for thereby some have entertained angels unawares.'"

She stared hard then laughed hard. "Are ya sayin' I might be an angel? First a rose and now an angel. Pete Blake, has anyone ever told you that you have a silver tongue?"

He blinked, then widened his eyes. "Of course not."

"Aye, someone should have by now."

He shook his head. But his eyes never left hers. Nor did she blink or turn away.

Neither spoke. The air between them was light, filled with words that spoke to her heart and to his as well, she hoped.

There was a sound somewhere. She couldn't say where, or even what it was. But it ended the moment. They continued on to the house.

"Did you have a good outing?" John asked; his attention on Eva.

His look and tone were so kindly, the words burst from her. "'T was lovely. Pete showed me a buffalo rub, a valley of trees in greens and golds and so many things. 'Tis a lovely country."

"I'm glad you enjoyed yourselves. And I agree. It's God's country."

"Aye?" Eva wasn't sure what he meant.

"John, you'll have her thinking God only dwells with people who live here." Maude gave Eva a kind smile. "What he means is the country is so pretty that it makes us feel like God has specially blessed us."

"That's what I mean." John and Maude smiled at each other, a look so intimate and full of familiarity that Eva felt she should look away, but she couldn't. That was the way it should be between a husband and wife. But only if they'd married for love. Not for convenience.

Not that she was complaining or regretting her decision. Like Mama said, 'The lines are fallen unto me in pleasant places.'

Scotty called them indoors for supper. The five of them sat around the table and after John prayed, they passed food from hand to hand. And such a bounty of food. Potatoes, carrots, turnips, gravy, meat—venison, she was told. It had an odd taste. So different than the fish she normally ate. But she liked it fine.

Scotty served rhubarb pie for dessert.

The meal over, she was about to offer to help clean up. After all, that was the agreement she'd made back at Fort Macleod. But Pete rose.

"If you'll excuse us, I want to show Eva around before it gets dark."

"Of course." John waved them away.

"I must help with dishes first," she protested.

"Nonsense," Maude said. "You are on your honeymoon until Monday. Only then will we allow you to help."

Eva felt the heat rush up her neck. She breathed slowly, deeply, in the hopes of discouraging the color she knew would be seeking a home in her cheeks.

"Thank you," she murmured, congratulating herself on speaking proper English. "Scotty, the meal was lovely. Thank you."

Pete took her hand and drew her out the back door. She'd never been on this side of the house and looked around. There was a chicken coop with clucking hens on one side. A fenced-in area to the other side.

"A garden?" she asked.

The dog, Ruff, lay on the veranda floor and lifted his head to look at them. Seeing they didn't bring food, he resumed his patient waiting.

"Yes, I'll show you," Pete said, drawing her down the steps.

She followed eagerly.

They reached the gate and leaned over it. She saw that much of it had already been harvested. Most of what remained were root vegetables and squash. And the last of peas and beans clinging to drying plants.

"We have to grow enough to last us the winter," he said. "Thankfully the weather has been good this year and the garden has done well." He told of the peas and beans that had been canned. The rhubarb, raspberries, and saskatoons that filled jars on shelves in the cellar of the house. "We'll dig the potatoes and carrots soon and put them in the root cellar. Come, I'll show you where it is."

They walked to the end of the garden and she saw the hill with a door in it. Pete opened the heavy door and she was assailed with the musty, dank odor.

There were bins along the walls and shelves mostly empty, though one shelf held a variety of pumpkin and squash.

Pete did a hard study of the door frame.

"Wou'd ya be lookin for something?" she asked.

"Herbie. But I see he hasn't returned."

She squinted at him. "And who would this Herbie be?"

"A garden spider."

She shuddered and drew back. "Och, a spider. How big?"

He circled his thumb and pointing finger. "About this big."

She backed up another step. "And this is his home?"

"Was. He got moved. I just wondered if he'd come back or stayed where he was put."

"Aye, and where was he put, pray tell?"

He turned, leaned on the door frame as if the thought of spiders crawling under his collar was'nae a problem.

She shuddered. "I dinna like spiders."

"Neither did Abby. She made Dillon move poor Herbie."

"Poor Herbie," she sputtered. "Aye, and is there something wrong with ye man to favor a spider? A big spider." She curled her finger and thumb together to illustrate what she meant.

"He's harmless. Catches flies and mosquitos. I say we should thank him."

"Och, no." She marched away.

He closed the door and hurried after her. "Eva, he now lives in the loft of the barn so he won't be bothering you."

She continued onward without responding.

"Are you upset?" he asked, puzzlement plain in his tone.

"I might have judged ya too soon."

"Huh?"

"Aye. Here I thought you were a perfect man. But no perfect man likes spiders."

He hooted with laughter.

She scowled at him. "'Tis not funny."

He managed to stop laughing for about three seconds then burst out again.

She planted her hands on her hips and gave him a look she hoped was scolding, disapproving. She should have the look perfected if only from seeing it on the faces of others. But his eyes were so full of amusement, his laugh round and echoing in her heart. She pursed her lips to hold back her own laugh.

He sobered enough to say. "Eva, I'm sorry to disappoint you but no man is perfect."

"Och, and could ya no'ave let me believe it for another day or two?"

His laugher died. His eyes grew serious. "Is that

what you are expecting? A perfect man? I confess I am not that, nor will I ever be."

The moment hung between them like a becalmed sail.

"I am already a disappointment to you."

8

Why did he let the idea of being a disappointment hurt so much? It wasn't as if he hadn't experienced that feeling before.

"Och, no, Pete." She clasped her hand to his upper arm.

He might have enjoyed the caress except for the sting of those words.

"Ya aren't a disappointment except in the spider matter and I will choose to overlook that small failing."

"Failing, is it now?" Her touch on his arm made the wound of her words close up like it had never occurred. "Tell me this, are all women afraid of spiders?"

"Och, I can't answer that. But ya tell me this. Are all men friendly to them?"

"Oh, I think so. We never had a problem with

Herbie before young women began appearing on the place."

"Appearing? How so?"

He drew her arm around his elbow and resumed walking along the trail that left the garden and building behind and climbed the nearby hill.

"Well, Maude found Abby stranded in Logan Crossing, about to have her baby. Mike brought Bethany here when his sister, Ilsa, had lost her home in Fort Calgary and he rescued them both. I told you how Noah found Lainie squatting on ranch land. Grace came to visit her brother Sam. She brought her friend, Yvette, with her."

"And now me."

He wasn't sure what to make of her response. "All most welcome, of course."

"Aye, of course."

They had reached the top of the hill and he drew her toward the bench sitting at the edge of the trees. "Let's sit."

They did. He wanted to say something to ease the tension he sensed in her.

"Eva, I am not regretting our decision to marry. I think we suit each other just fine." He waited, hoping she would give a satisfactory response.

She pressed her shoulder to his. "Aye, we do suit each other jest fine. I'll simply have to overlook your fondness for spiders." She faced him, her eyes steady, examining. "In return, I ask that you'll forgive me my failings."

He touched her cheeks. "I haven't seen any."

"Och, but ya will. Ya will."

"Then they are forgiven."

"But ya don't know what they are yet."

"I don't need to. I forgive them."

"I believe I've changed my mind."

His heart hit bottom with a thud that she surely must have heard.

"Aye, but you are the perfect man." She leaned back. "And aren't I the luckiest woman?"

He squeezed her hand. "And I the most fortunate man alive."

"Then it's settled? We are satisfied?"

"Very satisfied." And he'd choose to remain so even when he saw the others having babies and speaking of their love. It was more than he and Eva had bargained for and more than he could hope for.

They sat side by side as the sun lowered, tossing red and purple and pink banners across the sky. And they talked.

He told her of how Maude had picked him and Sam and Mike from the orphanage. And how she'd found Dillon broke and horseless, without even a pair of boots.

"His friend robbed him of everything in the night."

"Och, 'twas no friend."

"True. Maude found Noah and Adam trying to

scrape together a living after their step-father kicked them out."

"Aye, 'tis a sorry bunch ya were. Good thing Maude found ya all. I suppose I fit right in. Homeless, rejected by Mr. Sharp, not welcome at home."

"Why weren't you welcome?"

"It's as I told ya. I was blamed for me father's death at sea."

"I've said it before and I'll say it again. I'm sorry, but now you have a home here. Forever."

"Thank ya." She shifted so she could look him full in the face. "And I hope ya will find a home here." She pressed her hand to her chest then ducked her head as pink flooded her cheeks.

"Eva, the fact that you even want it is more than I ever expected." His words were husky; as if drawn through a long rough tunnel.

"Do ya mean from me or from life?"

"Yes."

She chuckled. "That's the way it is then?"

They sat back, shoulder to shoulder. For his part, he enjoyed the company more than the scene and the lowering sun.

He pointed out the location of Noah and Lainie's house. Thought of how much Noah enjoyed Lainie's brother and sister. "You met Boyd. He has a younger sister, Missy. She's seven. Both children are well behaved and fun to be around."

"I will meet them soon?"

"On Sunday. Remember how I told you we all get together to worship? I expect it will be a different experience for you. I didn't ask if you attended church in Pictou."

"Aye, we did. Pa had his regular pew and if anyone else sat there he would glower at them until they moved."

Pete thought her laugh lacked mirth.

"You brought your father's Bible. Did he read daily from it as John does?"

"I never saw him open the Good Book. He carried it to church. I think it 'twas to make everyone think he was pious and good."

Pete heard a note of pain in Eva's words. "Are you saying he wasn't?"

"Och, no. 'Tis wrong to speak ill of the dead. But," her voice lowered to a whisper. "Seems that goodness starts at home."

Pete took her hand. "I agree." She'd said enough that he understood her gentle, loving soul had been starved and bruised by her father's indifference. He would not be that way. Not that it was difficult to admire and appreciate her. "Eva, I hope you will find life better here. You will be treated kindly. And you will always be important."

She studied the far horizon. "I will work hard."

He knew immediately that she equated her importance with hard work. "No, that isn't what I meant." He took her hand between his. "Eva, in the few days

I've known you—" Was it really such a short time? He'd confessed more about his past to her than anyone here at the ranch. "In that time I've already learned to appreciate your sweet spirit and the way you enjoy life. If I could, I would find a way to make you laugh a hundred times a day just to see the joy in your face and hear your sweet laughter." His chest tightened. When had he ever been known to speak so freely and use such flowery words?

But it was worth it when she turned her face to him, full of joy.

"Pete, 'tis the nicest thing anyone has ever said to me. Ever."

But the source of those nice, flowery words had dried up and he couldn't find a single thing—flowery or otherwise—to say. Her eyes held his, making him feel adrift on a smooth lake, the realities of life far away.

She was the first one to move and with a sigh, sat back and leaned against his shoulder. "God has indeed put me in a pleasant place."

"God is good to us both."

They sat like that for some time, commenting about the changing colors in the sky until all that remained was a darkening blue.

He rose, took her hand, and led her back to the house.

John and Maude were inside waiting for him to help John to bed.

He'd plumb forgotten about his responsibilities. "I'm sorry. I should have been back sooner."

"It's early. We only just came inside. All too soon it will be too cold to sit out in the evenings," John reassured him.

Pete turned to Eva. "Go on up. I'll be there shortly."

Her gaze clung to him. If he read her correctly, she was reluctant to go without him. What a nice thought. To be wanted…needed…. He swallowed hard. Was it too much to expect that of their agreement?

She nodded, took a pitcher of warm water from the kitchen and went up the stairs.

Pete's gaze lingered on her until she was out of sight and then he hurried to assist John.

"What did she think of the country?" John asked as Pete helped him out of his day clothes and into his nightwear.

Pete assisted John in transferring from the wheelchair to the bed before he answered. "She seemed very impressed. Says she likes the wind and the sky."

John chuckled. "Then she's come to the right place." He caught Pete's hand before Pete could leave. "I hope she'll be very happy here and when you think the time is right, I hope you will tell me how you ended up marrying her." He spoke so kindly that Pete could not take offense at his words.

"I will." He said goodnight and hurried up the stairs. He could have said it was by the grace of God. There was no other way of explaining how both of them had been rejected by the one they thought they'd marry and then found each other. As Eva had said, 'The lines are fallen unto me in pleasant places.'

He entered the bedroom he now shared with Eva. His wife. She lay in bed propped up on one shoulder. Her hair was braided again. She wore a white nightgown. Her face seemed pinker than usual.

She noticed his study and touched her cheeks. "Too much sun."

"Do you have anything for it?"

"No."

"Hang on." He clattered back down the stairs and stopped outside John and Maude's room. "Maude, are you awake?" If not, he hoped he'd wakened her.

Maude stepped from the bedroom, still fully dressed. "Is there something wrong?"

He explained about Eva getting too much sun. "Do you have anything for it?"

"Her fair skin will burn easily. You better find her a wider brimmed hat when she's out riding. Now, come to the kitchen and I'll mix up something." She put some baking soda in a small bowl and added enough water to make a paste. "Put this on her face. Leave it ten minutes, then wash it off. That should help." She handed him the bowl.

He hurried upstairs with it. "Maude says this will help." He sat on the edge of her bed.

She shifted to make more room for him. "What are ya to do?"

"I'm to spread this on your cheeks." He dipped his finger into the paste, lifted it to her face and stopped. Her eyes were wide, full of uncertainty and expectation. She glanced away and then back to him. He felt her worry and fear. Felt her disappointment with life.

He didn't move, his hand suspended inches from her face.

Something shifted in her eyes. Acceptance? Dare he hope it was more?

He couldn't undo what had happened, couldn't erase her sorrow, but he could help her sunburn and he gently patted the paste on her cheeks, which were very warm.

She trembled but said nothing and didn't stop studying him with wide eyes. His fingers echoed her trembling.

He drew in a deep breath to steady his hand. And his nerves. He had every right to touch her. Had done so many times since they'd met. And married. There was no need for him to feel like his insides danced on a hot surface. But telling himself so didn't calm the sensation. He steeled his nerves into submission and continued applying the paste.

"Tomorrow, I will find you a hat with a broader brim."

"Thanks."

"There. That's done." He put the bowl to the side and sat back. "We're supposed to wait ten minutes or so, then wash it off."

"Aye." Her voice was soft, lazy. No doubt she was tired. That explained it. It would be foolish on his part to think his ministrations had lulled her into a state of contentment.

She continued to watch him until he looked away, unsettled by her study. What did she see? He had only to look in the mirror to know the answer. But he felt like she saw more than the color of his skin. It was as if she searched his thoughts. His very soul.

He shook his head. He was getting as foolish as an old man. Thinking he saw things when there was nothing to see.

Ten minutes wasn't a long time. The length of time it took to walk the perimeter of the home site. The amount of time it took to go to Noah and Lainie's place if one wasn't in a hurry. But today it slipped by with maddening slowness. He cleared his throat and looked at the wall behind Eva's head. Plaster painted pale green.

"We should hang a picture there. What would you like?"

She blinked, as if his words had awakened her, and turned to consider the wall he meant. "I dinna know."

"Did you bring any pictures from your home?"

She continued to study the blank wall. Then slowly settled back on her pillow without answering.

"Tell me what was on your walls back there. Something you liked."

Her eyes were shadowed. "There was nothing."

"Let's decide what *we* want then."

There was a moment of silence. Then she brightened and the light in her eyes lifted a heaviness that had filled the room.

"If I could paint, I would do a scene of the valley we saw. The ribbons of green and gold." She sighed. "But I cannae draw or paint so I will have to keep the picture up here." She tapped her head.

"We'll go there again soon."

"'Twould be pleasant to do so, but I haven't forgotten that I am here to work."

"And to enjoy life. And be my wife."

She stiffened. "Aye, I haven't forgotten a single thing we agreed to."

There was a warning note in her voice and he understood she feared he might have decided to change the terms of their agreement.

"Nor have I. Trust me. I am a man of my word."

The tension left her body. "'Tis good to know."

"It's time to wash that stuff off your face. Stay here and I'll get water and a cloth." He went to the next room, poured some warm water into the basin and returned with it. But when he tried to wipe her face with the damp cloth, she took it from him.

"I can do it."

He sat on the side of her bed and watched.

She rinsed the cloth several times as she cleaned her face. "I'm done." She dropped the cloth back in the basin.

"Not quite." He squeezed water from the cloth and gently wiped away the bits of white that she'd missed. His lungs were oddly reluctant to work. He hoped she wouldn't notice how jerky his hand was. The last spot was gone and he sat back. "Does it feel any better?"

"Aye. Thank ya." She yawned. "Och, I am sorry. I'm not used to being out so long."

He jumped to his feet. What was he thinking to be lingering on her bed? Keeping her from her sleep? "I'll go prepare for bed. You go to sleep." He rushed from the room.

"Och, no, I dinna mean to send you scurrying away."

He smiled as he washed up. He was far too ready to believe people didn't care for his company. She seemed determined to correct him of that notion. He was only too eager to hope she could.

He returned without any light and crawled under his covers as quietly as he could.

"Good night, my husband," she whispered.

"Good night, my wife." The words were like a blessing, a benediction on their agreement.

"Thank ya for the lovely day." Her whispered words were sweet to his heart.

"Thank you for making it lovely for me."

She chuckled softly. "'Twas my pleasure, for certain."

"Mine too."

She laughed again. "This could go on all night."

"Would that be so bad?" Having her so close and hearing her kind words might make it worthwhile to stay awake all night exchanging pleasantries.

"No. 'Twould be a pleasure. But if ya don't want me falling asleep in the middle of a sentence tomorrow I need to sleep." She added even more softly. "At least a few hours."

"Then you better go to sleep."

"Aye. Good night then."

He didn't answer, not wanting to keep her awake.

"Are ya asleep or angry at me?"

"I've decided not to answer you so you can go to sleep."

"Then why are ya talking to me?"

He heard the amusement in her voice and laughed. "Good night and it's the last time I'm going to say it."

"Forever?" The word was barely a breath.

He chuckled. "Go to sleep."

"Fine. I shall." He heard her shift on the bed. "Good night, Pete."

He laughed and turned on his side, toward her, though she probably couldn't tell in the darkness.

He could make out the shape of her under the covers. Words flitted through his head as he thought of the day they'd spent together. Pleasant was the first one. Fun. Interesting.

He didn't want to rob from the day he'd enjoyed, but how long before she realized it wasn't all fun and games? Before she encountered unkind remarks because of the color of his skin? And before she decided this was all a big mistake?

EVA COULD ALMOST HEAR Pete's thoughts. Worrying about what he'd gotten himself into marrying a girl like her. Fair skin that burned at the least hint of bright sun. She'd learned to wear a bonnet by the time she could walk. But it wasn't her hair or her skin that she worried he would find off-putting. It was her inability to curb her tongue. Hadn't Pa said it would be the death of her? She would try harder to stop blurting out everything.

She smiled into the darkness. Aye, but dinna it please her to tell him what she thought and see the surprise and pleasure in his eyes. Could be the man needed to hear the lovely things she saw in him.

Her palm lay beneath her cheek. She curled her fingers to the warm skin. Remembering how he'd put the paste on her burned cheeks, she felt heat pool at her hand. Not from too much sun, but from not enough Pete. Her longing for more of his touch had crashed over her like a rogue wave. Aye, it'd threatened to drown all reason, all memory of their agreement. Och, but he was a bonnie man in every way, and she would make him smile, praise his good deeds and do her very best to make him happy.

She eased one hand toward him. He would have to reach out to bridge the gap between them.

God bless this man of hers.

THE NEXT MORNING, Pete hurried her out to the barn as soon as she'd swallowed her last mouthful of coffee. She was'nae sure she'd ever enjoy the taste of the bitter brew but everyone else drank it and a large amount of cream made it go down without her grimacing.

"Can ya show me how to saddle Lady meself or is it too hard for the likes of me?" She gave him a cheeky grin.

He straightened, saw her smile, and smiled back. "I think the likes of you can do about anything you set your mind to."

"Aye, I'd do me very best."

"No one could ask for more. I certainly couldn't."

He had no idea how his words blessed her heart.

"Come here," he said. "First, you say hello to your horse...."

"Hello Lady, ya bonnie thing."

Pete chuckled. "A little bit of sweet talk can never go wrong either."

Aye, and might that not apply to both man and beast?

"Now the saddle blanket." He handed it to her and instructed her on where to place it. Step by step, he told her what to do. If she hesitated at any point, he reached out and guided her hand with his. She smiled to herself. All the more reason to hesitate.

Her horse ready, she stood by and watched him saddle his own mount. Watching was as good as doing. Better because, aye, she watched what he did, but she liked watching him even more.

He finished and came to her side. "You sure you're not too sore for more riding?" he asked.

Aye, she was sore, but it would take more'n that to make her miss another day alone with Pete. "Very sure."

He helped her to the back of her horse and they rode from the yard, a sack of food hanging from Pete's saddle. Today they rode west a short time then turned the opposite direction from where they'd gone yesterday. She dinna care where they went. Everything was new, but even more, she and Pete had the day to themselves. Another blissful sun-blessed day. Remembering what the sun did to her skin, she adjusted the wide-brimmed hat Pete had given her lower on her forehead.

"Would you like to see hoodoos?" he asked.

"Oh, aye, certainly." She paused. "What are hoodoos?"

"What if I said they were huge mountain men that are known for capturing innocent young women? Could be they would enjoy a redhead for a change."

She squinted at him. Was he serious? He stared ahead, not letting her see his eyes. Aye, but she knew he wou'nae take her to a place of danger. Not the Pete she knew.

A doubt flitted across her mind.

Did she know him?

She was learning to but no, he would not take her to such a place, but he might tease her. And she could tease him back.

"Aye, he'll have to get you first."

That brought his head around to look at her.

"Aye," she nodded, her expression appropriately sober, "because I am going to be behind you at all times."

"You'd throw me to the monsters?"

"I believe it is part of our marriage agreement."

"Love, honor, to have and to hold. I don't see anything in that about monsters."

"Dinna forget I also vowed to love, honor, and hold." Though she dinna remember the vows word for word, she knew she'd sworn before God until death do them part. "And I mean to hold you in front of me if we see any monsters."

He stared at her. Must have seen the humor in her eyes she couldn't stifle. And then he burst out laughing. Great rolling roaring laughs that echoed off the rocks.

She grinned, satisfied at having amused him.

He shook his head, pretending to be sad. "Your friends back east must really miss you."

"Friends? Aye."

He rode closer and stopped his horse. "Are you saying you didn't have friends? That's not possible."

"You are a dear man for thinking so." She shrugged. "I've had friends."

His eyebrows rose, asking for an explanation.

"Allie was my friend. Her mama was dead and her grannie dinna care if she spent time with me. Och, the fun we had racing over sandy beaches and collecting shells. Sometimes Mama would give us a lunch and let us go down to the beach for the day." She sighed. Memories are both sweet and bitter.

"You must miss Allie and she must miss you."

"She moved away almost two years ago. Her grannie died and her father sent her to live with an aunt in Toronto. And aye, I miss her more than words can tell."

"You must have had other friends. In fact, I can't imagine that a dozen young men and women didn't compete to spend time with you."

She shrugged.

They rode on at a slow pace.

"No beaus?" Pete asked after a bit.

He had every right to ask. And to get an answer. But speaking the truth opened up a barely-healed wound. "I once liked a boy. Thought he liked me."

"What was his name?"

"Clyde."

"Noble sounding name."

"Aye." She filled her reluctant lungs. "And dinna I once think so?"

"What happened?"

"After Pa drowned, Clyde's mother said I was bad luck and he must stay away."

Pete edged closer and squeezed her arm. "It's not true. You are my lucky copper penny."

She laughed. "A penny, is it?" A penny might not be worth much, but his words pleased her.

He tipped his head and studied her. "Were you the only redhead person there?"

"No. There were more. Why?"

"I'm trying to understand why you were judged for the color of your hair if you weren't the only one."

"'T was more for my wild ways." To her shock, she'd learned there was even more than that. But that news would stay back in Pictou.

They had been climbing and she stared at the sight below them.

"What are those strange things?" They looked like huge men. She shuddered. "I thought you were fooling about the mountain men." Her heart racing madly, she reined Lady around. "Let's get out of here."

9

"Whoa." Pete reached for Lady's bridle and stopped her. "No one is going to hurt you."

She looked at him with big eyes.

"Eva, those are hoodoos. A rock formation. Have a look."

She shifted her gaze from him.

Reluctantly, he thought. Perhaps afraid if she took her eyes off him, danger would befall her. "I wouldn't let anything happen to you."

Her gaze returned to his. "Hoodoos?" The word whispered from her lips.

"Funny-shaped rocks."

She nodded. "No danger?"

"None. Though, I've heard it said if you sleep under them the rocks will fall on you."

"I shall remember that."

"Do you want to see them closer?"

"Och, no. I think I see them well enough from here."

He chuckled. "Better safe than sorry?"

"Aye."

"Then we'll go that way." He pointed to the right and they rode on. His mind was a whirl of thoughts. Why had she been so shunned back East? It didn't seem her coloring was that unusual. But he felt her pain every time she talked about life where she'd grown up. He wished he knew what caused her so much grief. But it seemed to hurt her to talk about it, so he would let it go.

"We can walk from here." He helped her down, noting that it took her a few minutes to get her legs steady. But he knew she'd resist any suggestion that they cut short the outing. He tied the horses and took her hand, leading her up the steep path. The trail was overgrown with bushes that he parted to enable them to continue.

"Where are ya taking me?" she asked.

"There is a secret cave ahead."

She stopped, pulling on his hand to stop him. "Secret? Then ya cannae show me."

"You are part of the Circle A now so it's your secret too." Besides, he wanted her to know everything about him…of course, he meant the ranch.

But did he?

There was something about Eva that made him want to put his heart in her hands. Or had he already done so by marrying her? It didn't matter the how or when. Enough that, for the first time since he was very young, he discovered he not only wanted to share every aspect of his life with her, but he was willing, even eager, to trust her. Perhaps he could finally leave behind the pain of his early life and, as she'd said, forget the past and look to the future.

"Part of the Circle A, ya say?" She shook her head. "No, 'tis not so."

Her words jerked through his head. "Of course you are. As my wife." Soon, he knew, she'd find herself part of the larger family that made up the dwellers of the ranch. But today and tomorrow, she was his alone. "Come on, Eva, let me show you the cave."

She nodded and let him guide her onward.

"We're here."

"Aye, in the middle of nowhere with nothin' but trees and bushes and rocks to look at."

He chuckled at her dry tone. "That, my dear wife, is why the cave is secret."

The words 'dear wife' had come unbidden, unconsidered, but oh so naturally. She blinked, as surprised by them as he was. Her gaze held his, searching, questioning. He let her see the answers he hoped she sought. He'd called her dear because she was. Dear in actions. Dear in thoughts and most of all, dear to his heart.

Not that he could explain to anyone what he meant. Or justify how it was possible in such a short time. Except it was and had been from the moment he sat beside her at the train station and heard her story and realized he could help her.

Her eyes were shaded by her hat. He tipped it back to better read her expression. His fingers brushed across her warm cheek.

Her freckles blazed, backlit by a gentle blush. Her expression cleared, her eyes captured the blue of the sky. And she smiled.

"Then, dear husband, reveal this secret cave."

Pete no longer cared about the cave. It would be there tomorrow, next week, and years in the future. Unlike this fragile moment. If he didn't capture the feeling that hung between them like a fluttering butterfly, it might well disappear and never return.

"Dear husband, is it?" His voice sounded as if rocks rumbled down his throat.

"'Tis. And is it dear wife?"

"It is." He cupped his hand to the back of her head. "I want to kiss my dear wife."

"Aye, and what, pray tell, is stoppin' ya?"

"Nothing. Not one thing."

"All talk and no action." She lifted her face to him and he wasted no time in accepting her invitation. He kissed her warm, sweet lips.

Roses, honey, and sunshine filled his thoughts and washed his heart.

She sighed against his lips, tickling them.

He lifted his head and looked into her eyes. "That was nice."

"Nice? No, 'tis too plain a word."

He smiled, pleased at her reaction. "What word would you use?"

"Och, bonnie sweet, like heaven leaned down and touched our lips."

He hugged her. "Eva, heaven surely had a hand in bringing you to me."

She leaned back, grinning up at him. "And here I thought 'twas the other way around. Heaven brought you to me."

Laughter bubbled up from deep inside him, from a spot that had, until now, been locked and barren. A spot where nothing but joy and contentment, with a large dose of humor, lived.

She laughed too.

He couldn't say the source of her amusement, but perhaps it was the same as his. An unfamiliar and yet, at the same time, familiar feeling. One that had lain dormant in his heart for years.

What was its source for her? Perhaps simply knowing he accepted her—freckles and all.

The trees above them rustled with birds.

He remembered they were there to see the cave and parted the thicket of bushes at his side to reveal an opening into the side of the hill.

She gasped.

He drew her back, knowing that small animals and

bats often exited when light blasted into their quarters. But nothing moved. "Shall we?" He waved his hand toward the opening.

She drew back. "It looks dark."

"We'll stay forward so we're in the light."

"Aye."

He took that for agreement to enter. The opening was too small for them to go side by side, so he led the way, tucking her behind him, prepared to defend her against any attack from in front.

They stepped into the first room with a high ceiling and stalactites hanging from the roof.

She moved to his side, clinging to his hand.

He hoped it was as much from wanting to be connected to him as wanting his protection.

"'Tis big." She shivered. "And cold."

"We have often camped here. The six of us. The first time we had only been here a few months and Maude sent us up. Told us it was time we learned to work together and survive without anyone telling us what to do." He chuckled at the memory.

"The first day there was some jockeying about as to who was going to boss who around. Dillon, being the oldest, appointed himself in charge. But Noah objected to it. Said he and Adam had managed on their own without a boss, thank you very much. Sam, well, he would agree to anything, but he wasn't going to choose sides. Poor Mike tried to reason with them that wasting time and energy on arguing and lifting their fists was foolish."

She tipped her head and studied him. "What did ya do?"

He grinned. "I went out and gathered wood, built a fire." He pointed to the spot where they always lit the wood. "I put my bedroll in the spot where I expected to sleep then left to get water. There's a stream just below us.

"When I got back, the others had put out their bedrolls and set about making camp. I don't know what was said. Never asked."

She tucked her hands around his arm and pressed her face to his shoulder. "Good on ya for settin' a fine example."

"All I knew was Maude expected us to stay a week and I meant to enjoy the time."

"A week? Sounds like a long time."

"It was good for us. We explored every inch of this hill and beyond. We had horse races and foot races and played games. You probably think we were too old to play, but I think it was good for us. I know, for me, it made me remember that life is fun. Oh, and we hunted. Managed to bring down a deer, so we ate like kings."

"It sounds like a lot of fun."

"It was." He remembered what she'd said about wandering on the beach. "Maybe not unlike some of the things you liked to do."

"Aye?"

"Yes, you talk about how you enjoyed being free."

"Och, and isn't it one of the things I was judged for?"

"I can't imagine why." He led her from the cave and up the hill to the very crest and indicated they should sit. Before them lay a view of rolling hills and beyond that prairie land that went on and on into the distance.

"I thought the ocean was big," she said after studying the scene. "But never did I see so far. 'Tis glorious."

"Yes, it is. I come here often."

"I can see why. The mountains make me think of God as strong and mighty. But these never-ending grasslands make me think of Him as vast beyond all measure. His love touching the earth and reaching beyond the clouds."

The power of her words spoke to his heart. "I guess that's why I come here when I'm troubled."

She slowly brought her gaze from the scene to his face. "And what troubles ya, my dear husband?"

"Not everyone sees me as dear. Often they see a man with dark skin who doesn't know who his parents are. That is too much for many." He knew she'd understand about people objecting to one's coloring, but at least she knew who her parents were. Not that any of that mattered anymore. Eva had married him, had promised to stay with him no matter what and that gave him a sense of belonging like nothing else had.

"Aye, some people see with their eyes but not their heart."

"What do you mean?"

"If they saw with their hearts, they would see that you are a good man. One they'd count themselves fortunate to know."

"Thank you for saying that."

"'Tis but the truth."

They fell into a comfortable silence as they looked out over the scene.

She sighed softly. "Makes me think of dreams."

"Dreams?" The word caught him off guard. He wasn't one to dream—either in sleep or in life. "What sort of dreams?"

EVA COULD HAVE BITTEN her tongue for speaking without thinking. The time for dreams was over. 'Twas time to be living her decision. Her choice. Not that she regretted marrying Pete. Not for one moment. But it did put an end to one dream she'd carried in the bottom of her heart since she was a child.

She felt his patient waiting as she struggled to think how to answer him. "I was an only child."

"So I understood."

"'Tis lonely with no brothers or sisters."

"Uh-huh."

She couldn't tell if he agreed or disagreed. "You had lots of others around in the orphanage and now you have so many people here. Like family."

"They *are* family and now you have them too."

She nodded. There was no point in saying her dream had been to have a dozen children, playing happily around her. Oh, and wouldn't she read to them, play with them, teach them the things they needed to know?

He took her silence for uncertainty. "I know they're all strangers right now, but it won't take long for them to all become good friends."

"Aye."

"Is that your only dream? To be part of a big family?"

She silently, determinedly buried the dream of children. It must be forever forgotten. "Aye." And lest he ask more questions, she turned to him. "And what's your dream?"

He turned away, but not before she caught a darkness rushing into his eyes. "I don't dream. I'm satisfied with the present."

He might think he was being matter-of-fact and all, but dinna she hear pain in his voice? "Pete, I'm sorry."

"Sorry? Why? I just said I'm content."

"Aye, your words said that. Your tone said elsewise."

He shook his head. "You heard wrong."

She knew she hadn't and her heart beat regret to know he wasn't willing to tell her. Whatever his dream had been, he'd given up on it. 'T was sad.

"Let's go back to the horses and get the lunch Scotty made." Pete pulled her to her feet and they scrambled down the hill to where the horses were tied. He got the sack of food and led her to the stream of water where they sat to eat.

"Is there something, in particular, you'd like to see, or a place you'd like to go?"

"Aye. I would like to see the cows and understand what it is you do."

"We can do that this afternoon."

"Ah, thank you. It is good of John and Maude to give us these few days."

"Our honeymoon?" He kept his gaze fastened on the sandwiches Scotty had prepared for them.

She laughed a little, knowing it sounded strangled. This was not what others would think of as a honeymoon. And yet— "'Tis nice to have time to get to know you better and see the place that is to be my home."

He met her gaze. His eyes were dark and bottomless, making her feel like she had gained wings and the ability to fly. "It's been good, hasn't it?" he said.

"Aye. Very good." She wished it could last longer, but they still had the rest of today and all of tomorrow. She would think no farther than that.

They took their time eating. Conversation

included him identifying the birds they saw. He told how John read aloud to them in the winter months.

"I suppose that will end now that everyone has their own home."

"Will we not be living with John and Maude?" she asked, surprised at his announcement.

"Of course. Now you've caused me to think of my dream."

"Aye?" She sat up straighter and focused her attention on him. "And it is?"

"They've given me about the only home I've ever known and my dream and hope is I can stay with them and assist them as long as they live."

"'Tis a noble dream." Yet for some reason, it disappointed her. Maybe because she wasn't part of it. But then, she dinna speak of him in her wishes for the future. Even though in her mind, he was bigger than life, larger than dreams, and warmer than sunshine. Or might it be that she sensed this dream was not the first one that came to his mind? "John and Maude are very generous."

"We—all of us including you—are their family. They had a son, Eddie. They built the ranch in hopes of him joining them and beginning a long line of Arbuckles on the ranch."

"What happened to that dream?"

"Eddie was killed in a robbery before he got here."

"And then John was crippled. So much tragedy. 'Tis sad."

"But they both believe that God has turned it to their good. Now they have six sons. They call us sons. And now daughters-in-law and grandchildren. They would say they are blessed."

Grandchildren. But not hers and Pete's. Not according to their agreement.

And yet hadn't he kissed her? And found her a willing party to it? And hadn't it felt good and right? Och, yes it had. But with kissing and hand-holding she must be content.

They finished the lunch and rode onward. She was about to see what being a cowboy was about. "'Tis not that I haven't seen cows ya know?"

"I didn't think it was. You couldn't have traveled most of the continent and not seen herds of cows and horses."

"I also saw three bears and a moose. And dinna a moose have a big hat to carry about?"

He laughed. "You could say that."

"Aye, and I just did."

He slanted an amused grin at her. "So you did."

Her grin lasted until they drew to a stop on a rolling hill.

"There's part of the herd." Pete pointed.

Below them, scattered like random rocks on the grass, were cows. Brown and black and a combination of both. A few sat on the ground. Smaller ones chased each other.

"Aye, but where are the cowboys?" She dinna have

the faintest notion of what the men would do. "Seems the cows manage just fine on their own."

"Did you think we had to spoon-feed them?"

She might have been offended, but she heard the teasing in his voice. "Aye. Only you'd use a fork."

He grinned at her. Then his attention returned to the cows. "There." He pointed. "It's Noah driving back a bunch of strays."

She followed the direction he pointed and squinted, barely able to make out the rider behind the cows. "It takes five men to do that?" Surprise colored her words. She cou'nae even say what she expected, but this was'nae it.

"Eva, we ride a large area, watching for wayward cows. Sometimes there are sick or injured ones to take care of. We keep an eye open for bears or mountain lions or even wolves who would enjoy a good beef dinner."

She gulped. "Wild animals?"

"They aren't uncommon this close to the mountains."

"And ya say it like you announced the sun was peeking over the edge of the earth. I suppose you'll be a cowboy again soon. How do ya expect me to sleep when I know there are bears and wolves out here looking for their dinner? Don't suppose they care if it's cow or man." She made no attempt to keep the annoyance and fear out of her words.

"In seven years, not a scratch. See for yourself." He held out his hands, inviting her inspection.

She glowered at him, though her look was likely more pleading with a touch of fear. "And isn't there a first time for everything?"

He caught her hands. "Eva, I am always careful, and now with a wife to return to, I'll be even more cautious."

She nodded, though his words did little to comfort her.

He released her hands and indicated she should follow him down the hill. They rode toward the cows.

She glanced from side to side, seeing a wild animal in every shadow.

"Eva, you are perfectly safe. There are no wild animals around here."

"If ya say so." But she didn't stop staring at the trees which, in her mind, provided a perfect place for an animal to lay in wait.

Pete chuckled. "Maybe I'll have to teach you how to shoot a gun."

Eva shuddered. "Och, no. But I might welcome a sword."

Pete laughed like she'd hit a particularly funny spot.

She wasn't sure what was so funny, but it was good to hear him laugh.

They stopped riding again. "There's the chuckwagon," he said, pointing. "Do you want to meet Sam and the others?"

"No, not today." She wanted to spend her time with Pete alone. Dinna fancy having to meet the others any sooner than she must.

A fire burned with pots hanging over it. "Looks like Sam is the cook," Pete said. "Scotty used to cook for us, but he did his best to teach us how to manage on our own. Now he only comes out occasionally."

"Ya can cook?" There was so much she didn't know about this man.

"Basic things. Not like Scotty."

"'Tis good to know. I dinna think I want to be a worse cook than my husband."

"I don't think that's possible."

He described how meals were prepared outdoors, pointed out the rope corral for spare horses, told about the things they'd had to deal with as a cowboy. Floods, cows stuck in the mud, a draw blocked by falling earth that required they dig out the passageway.

Eva listened, fascinated with the work Pete did.

"Ya say ya are going to go back to the cows. Who is going to look after John?"

"We take turns. The married ones go to their own homes at night but help with getting him up and preparing him for bed. If he needs help throughout the day, someone is nearby."

Eva turned her horse about. She didn't want to

think of Pete leaving her even if it was to do his job. A huge hole, the size of the cave, consumed her insides at the mere idea.

Pete joined her and they rode slowly in the general direction of the ranch. Seems he was in no more hurry to get back than she.

If she could, she would not return. She chuckled.

Och, and dinna that make him give her a questioning look.

"Care to share what's amusing you?" he said.

"'Tis silly, but aye, I'll tell ya." She repeated what she'd thought. "I might think it's what I want, but truth be told, I like a soft bed and a roof over my head."

He edged his horse closer and covered her hands with his. "Eva, I know everything is new and strange for you, but it will get easier. I promise. I don't think I'll have any trouble convincing John to let me spend another week at home."

"I dinna want to be the cause of discord between you and the others."

"You won't be." He pointed to a patch of bright yellow flowers and they rode closer and dismounted.

Her legs were so sore that she clung to him for several minutes. She dinna mind the excuse. But she dinna need one, did she? They were husband and wife. That gave her the right to hold him whenever it suited her. And to kiss him, if she took the notion. And she took it now.

She stretched up on her tiptoes and brushed her lips to his. They were warm with the sun.

He held her, staring into her eyes. "What was that?"

"Och, and dinna ya know a kiss when ya get one?"

"I sure do." He bent and kissed her in a way she'd never before been kissed. Gentle, claiming, lingering, promising.

Promising? They had given their promises when they married. She cou'nae ask for more.

He lifted his head.

She swallowed hard. "Aye, you surely do know what a kiss is."

He laughed softly. "Better than I knew."

Heat rushed up her cheeks. And she cou'nae blame it on the sun. She shifted her gaze past his shoulder. "Flowers." She'd plumb forgotten that was their reason for this detour and broke from his arms to run to the sunflower-like blossoms. Only they dinna have the yellow face of a sunflower. The center resembled a pine cone. Yellow petals hung from the cone. "Like a lady dancing in her summer gown," she said.

He sat beside her. "You make me see flowers in a different way."

"Aye? How so?"

"Before now they've just been flowers. Different colors and some, like roses, smell better. But I've never thought of them as dancing."

"No?" She broke the stem of two and held one in each hand. She made the first bow and join the other and then she made them dance, humming a tune as she did so. Suddenly, she realized how silly she must look and stopped the music. Stopped the dance. Swallowed hard. But she kept the flowers. 'T would be a waste to throw them away.

Pete must have sensed her embarrassment for he reached out an arm to her. It put him off balance and he fell to his back, pulling her down beside him.

Her first instinct was to bolt to her feet, flip over like a landed fish. But then she reminded herself, aye, and wasn't she his wife and had every right to lie next to him, his arm under her shoulders. And no one should complain or criticize.

So she stayed still. Felt his chest rising and falling. Felt the warmth of his body against hers. Heard the ache of her insides as she wished she hadn't agreed to be wife in name only.

But she wou'nae cry over spilt milk. Or moan about something she cou'nae change.

What was it her pa often said when he felt someone had given up on a task too soon? *A coward gives up. A man dinna quit ever.* She was'nae a man, but neither was she a coward. And when it came to stubbornness and perseverance, she was as good as any man. Better'n some, she decided, thinking of Mr. Sharp.

She might not get all she wanted in this marriage she'd agreed to, but she'd get enough to satisfy her. Who could ask for more than a good man? He made her laugh. He dinna mind her red hair and freckles. He was kind. And listened to her babble without complaint.

She pushed aside even the hint of regret. She would be the best wife Pete could want and do him proud in her work.

If she ever felt regretful, she would take herself out for a walk and fill her thoughts with the beauty of the countryside.

If she dinna find that enough it was her own failing.

10

Eva lay at Pete's side. She'd made no attempt to move away as if perfectly comfortable with the situation. Pete ignored the rock jabbing into his back and the awkward angle of his arm as it lay under Eva's shoulders. Not for one ounce of comfort would he end this moment of sweetness and connection between them.

John and Maude had been right and wise in giving Pete and Eva these few days together. Otherwise, they would have gone about their work, seeing each other at mealtimes and bedtime. This time of getting to know her was a pleasant interlude. She surprised him in so many ways. Full of fun and laughter. And—remembering how she'd kissed him—given to bits of boldness. Which, he admitted with a pleased smile—suited him just fine.

She shifted up on her elbow and looked down at him.

He wondered what she wanted until she drew a feathery head of grass across his face and laughed as he brushed it away. He caught her hand and pulled her down until she lay on his chest, one elbow digging into his ribs.

Her gaze was molten blue, full of sunshine heat, drawing him from himself into something bigger, sweeter—

Riskier.

He'd long ago locked his heart behind immovable barriers. He meant to keep it that way. He'd let her in, but only as far as that barrier.

Her look grew warmer, full of invitation. Her gaze went to his mouth and stalled there.

He knew what she wanted and wasn't opposed to giving it. He pulled her down and claimed her lips. They lingered, exploring. The barrier in his heart shook. Rocked back and forth. It wouldn't take much to topple it.

Something crawled up his cheek. He swatted it away.

She sat back at the interruption. Looked at him. "Ants." She was instantly on her feet and shaking her skirt, brushing her hands over her arms.

He jumped up and scrubbed ants off his shirt. He turned. "Are there any on my back?"

"Och, everywhere." She brushed at his back. "You must have laid on an anthill."

"Let's get out of here." He grabbed her hand and they raced away, stopping twice to brush off more ants.

They returned to the horses who grazed contentedly nearby.

She started to laugh. "Wolves and bears and now ants. What next? Wee little men creeping out from behind the rocks?" She sobered and looked past him. Her eyes grew round. Her lips parted as if she wanted to say something, but no words came out. She jabbed one finger in the direction she looked.

What did she see? He turned slowly, his fists up, his stance wide, prepared for anything. Apart from the flowers where they'd recently laid and the grass and nearby trees, he failed to see anything of concern. He narrowed his eyes, searching the trees. "I don't see anything." He turned back to her.

She covered her mouth stifling her laughter. Her eyes flashed. "Gotcha," she choked out and released her merriment in great gulps of laughter.

He glowered, and stalked toward her. "Have you heard of the boy who cried wolf?"

"Aye." She sobered, but her eyes told him she was still laughing on the inside. "And should I be saying I'm sorry?"

"Only if you mean it." They were toe to toe now.

"'Twas only in fun. Besides, I dinna say there was

something out there, now did I?"

"I guess you didn't but—"

She didn't give him time to finish. "Aye, then I dinna cry wolf."

He shook his head in mock frustration. "What am I going to do with you?" Besides enjoy her company and be grateful they'd found each other.

She clasped her arms around his neck. "You could try kissing yer wife again."

He touched his lips to hers, intending only for a quick kiss, but she pulled his head down and the short kiss grew into a deep, lingering one. With a groan, he stepped back.

How was he to keep his promise to have a marriage in name only if she kept doing this? How was he to keep that barrier in place around his heart when being with her made it tremble? When kissing her shook him to the core?

The best way was to keep busy, keep moving, keep talking.

He helped her to the back of her horse and they rode toward the ranch. He didn't realize how long he'd been quiet until Eva spoke.

"Are ya angry with me?" Her voice was soft, her words uncertain.

"No, of course not."

"I dinna mean to be so foolish."

Her injured tone was his undoing. He reined in close to her and reached for her hands. "It is I who should apologize for making you think I am offended. It was a harmless trick and a good one at that."

She nodded. "Are we all right then?"

"We are very all right." He resumed the journey toward home. Spoke softly, "Just don't do it again." He fully intended she should hear and hoped she'd take it as teasing.

She sighed expansively. "Och, and there goes all my fun."

"Oh, I'm sure you'll find other ways to keep me on my toes."

"Aye. That I will."

"Good."

They grinned at each other. She seemed happy with the idea. He knew he was. Life with Eva promised lots of fun and laughs.

They returned to the ranch, took care of the horses, working together like they'd been doing so for years. Except for the time she stepped in front of him, blocking his path and demanding a kiss to get out of his way. He pretended to be annoyed. Made as if to move her aside without paying her toll, but even knowing every kiss whittled away at his protective walls, he gave one willingly.

They joined John and Maude, who still sat outside.

"What did you see today, Eva?" John asked.

"A cave, the cows, and maybe forever."

John chuckled. Pete saw the approving look in the older man's gaze. "You aren't the first one to feel that when they see the vast plains spread out as far as the eye can see."

"Aye, and some yellow flowers." She slanted a look at Pete, her eyes twinkling with remembrance.

He swallowed audibly and turned toward the kitchen door. "Is supper ready?" He might have thought his reaction hadn't been noticed, but John chuckled again.

"Seems like the day was satisfactory."

"Aye."

Did anyone but Pete hear the pleased note in her voice?

Scotty yelled, "Come and get it before I throw it to the dog."

Pete stepped back to let Maude and John go first, then smiled at Eva and followed her inside.

Conversation at the meal was mostly about plans for the construction of the schoolhouse. John wanted a crew to work on it. Pete hoped that meant he'd be staying around the place for a time. He normally enjoyed being out with the cows, spending hours alone as he rode up one draw after another. But now the idea held no appeal.

After the meal was over and Eva's offer to help had been rejected, he asked her to walk with him. He had nothing in mind but spending the evening with her. They made their way to the bench and sat.

"I feel guilty not helping," she said.

He took her hand. "You'll get plenty of chance."

Another thought crossed his mind. "Are you not enjoying a few days of play?" With him?

She leaned against his shoulder. "Och, ya dinna need to ask. Of course, I am enjoying your company."

That wasn't what he'd asked, but it was what he wanted to know. How had she known?

The sun dipped toward the west and, wanting her to enjoy the sunset, he led her to the crest of the hill and they sat on the grass to watch as the sky filled with unbelievable pinks and oranges and the sun became a gold rim along the top of the mountains.

"'Tis beautiful. 'The lines are fallen unto me in pleasant places.'"

Her words warmed his insides, but he couldn't think of any words of his own to describe what he felt so only said, "I'm glad you think so."

They stayed until the color was reduced to a pale pink, then they hurried back.

She went upstairs while he helped John prepare for bed.

"Pete," John said. "I like what I see of Eva. She is the perfect match for you. Light-hearted and open about her feelings. I believe she'll be good for you."

"I agree." He felt John's curiosity but didn't explain how he'd met Eva. Unless she chose to reveal the story, it would remain their secret. "Can I borrow the wagon tomorrow?"

"I don't think it's needed for anything, so by all means."

Pete appreciated that John didn't ask what Pete planned that required a wagon. He wanted it to be an outing for just him and Eva. Maybe John was right. Pete liked to keep his thoughts, plans, and feelings to himself.

He finished with John and took the stairs three at a time. He slowed his steps and his heart before he stepped into the bedroom.

Eva was already in bed as he'd expected. "I won't be long," he said as he went to the other room to prepare for nighttime.

When he returned, she lay on her side, one hand beneath her cheek. Her eyelids didn't even flutter. The poor girl was exhausted by so much riding. He slipped quietly into bed and lay on his back.

He reached out one hand. Couldn't quite reach the other bed. So close and yet so far.

Kind of like their marriage.

Eva looked at the wagon. A tarpaulin covered something in the back. "Where are we going?" she asked Pete.

"It's a surprise."

"I dinna like surprises." She gave him a look she hoped told him she was strongly opposed to them.

"Too bad. I guess you'll have to trust me on this."

They faced each other. Neither moved toward

getting on with this journey.

Aware that John and Maude watched from the veranda, Eva rolled her eyes. "Very well."

Grinning, he helped her up to the wagon seat then planted himself beside her.

"Ya dinna need to look so pleased with yerself."

He laughed. The sound of his low, delighted laugh bubbled inside her like a gushing fountain. She laughed along with him. They waved to John and Maude and drove off in the opposite direction of the previous two days.

She looked about, keenly interested in everything.

They traveled for some time along a rough trail, much of the time close to a stream that gurgled over rocks.

"Logan Creek," Pete said. "Though John says it's really a river. It flows year long. Floods from time to time with the spring melt."

"'Tis different than the rivers that flow into Pictou Harbor. They are deep and appear to be slow-moving, but dinna be misled."

"Rivers? As in more than one?"

"Aye, the East River, the West River, and the Middle River." She laughed, amused as always that the names were so plain. "How did Logan Creek get its name?"

"An early explorer by the name of Logan camped here. Named the river after himself."

They left the trail, heading toward some trees. He

stopped the wagon. "We're here."

"Aye?"

"Come on. I'll show you."

She had no objection to following him, wherever he might lead.

They passed through the trees to a sandy bank along the creek.

"We're going there." He indicated the spot below them.

"Aye?"

"Come on, help me carry our supplies." They returned to the wagon. He lifted the canvas to reveal a familiar-looking sack. Scotty had again provided food. There was also a cast iron fry pan, fishing rods, quilts—

"How long are we staying?" she asked.

"As long as we like."

She chuckled. "Think we might be needing more than this to stay here forever."

He laughed and handed her the quilts and fishing rods. He carried the rest of the supplies and they returned, slid down the embankment and deposited their things at the foot of the sandy bank. The nearby water was a calm pool diverted from the rushing current.

He arranged everything to his satisfaction, then took up the fishing rods and baited the hooks.

She watched.

"You ever been fishing?" he asked.

"Maybe. Sort of. Allie found an old fishing rod in her grannie's attic and we tried fishing but didn't have the patience to wait for a fish to come along."

"Didn't you ever go with your father?"

"Och, no. 'Twould be bad luck to for him to take me out with him."

He cast a line into the water and then handed her the pole. "Let it drift a bit, then reel it in and cast it again." He put his own line in the water.

She imitated him as he played the line in the water, slowly reeling it in and then casting it again.

She tried and the lure stalled in midair.

He showed her again how to do it and she succeeded on the third try. She didn't crow, but she was pleased with her success.

Her line tightened.

"You have a fish." He spoke calmly.

"I dinna know what to do." Panic laced her words.

"Hang on, I'll show you." He put his rod down and, reaching his arms around her from the back, guided her in reeling in a fish. He unhooked it from the line and put it in a basket. "Good job, Eva. You caught a fish."

In a short time, she caught another and reeled it in on her own. He caught three.

"Maybe I'm not bad luck after all," she said.

They took a break from fishing and sat with their backs to the sandy bank.

He opened the sack of food and handed her three

molasses cookies.

Their shoulders pressed together. His jean-clad legs stretched out. She curled her legs under her gray skirt. The movement put more pressure on her shoulder against Pete. He shifted to better accommodate her.

They sat in companionable silence, eating their cookies.

"You most certainly aren't bad luck."

His statement startled her. She'd forgotten her careless remark. "Can ya be certain?" She turned her face to him, wanting…not sure what she wanted. Or was she denying the longing in her heart that had existed since she could remember?

"I am certain sure." He smiled—as much with his eyes as with his mouth.

She sat back. What if…? What if he found out the truth about her? But how could he? No one here knew. No one back east cared where she was. But the burden of keeping back part of herself and the truth weighed on her like a house-sized boulder.

"Pete, ya dinna know about me."

There must have been something in her tone that alerted him. He shifted and looked into her face.

"I can't imagine there is anything about you that would make me think less of you."

"You cannae be certain."

He put his arms around her. "Whatever it is, it won't change things. We are married and I intend to keep my vows. My feelings for you are bound by those vows."

She wasn't sure what he meant. That only the words spoken back in Fort Macleod would keep him married to her? Well, it was what she had agreed to as well. "I mean to keep my vows as well. 'T will be my pleasure."

"Then we are agreed." He leaned back, one arm remaining across her shoulders. Would that arm also be removed if he knew the truth?

"I have a secret," she said, her words barely audible. "I don't have to tell you and you'd likely never find out, but I find it a burdensome weight."

He squeezed her tighter to his side. "Don't be afraid to tell me."

"Very well." She clasped her hands together and stared straight ahead. "You have to understand that I dinna know this until my father drowned. Though it explains why I was shunned and considered bad luck." Her throat stiffened and she forced herself to take deep breaths until it loosened.

"It also explains why my father ignored me and pushed me away. Och, I loved him and wanted him to love me back, but 'twas impossible."

Pete waited as she struggled with her words. His arm held her to his side, but the warmth of his body did nothing to ease the chill gripping her insides.

She continued. "People helped lay Father away after he drowned. Then they slipped off. I have never felt so alone. No one to hold me when I cried." She sniffed. The time for crying was past. Long past. "I tried to keep on. But the money soon ran out and no one would help me. No one would hire me. Not even to clean fish."

Both Pete's arms came around her and he pressed her to his chest. But she forced herself to sit up. Though she did not shake off his arm around her back.

"I'd overheard gossip about me. That Father died because I was willful. Wild. I should have stayed home and made the place happy for my father. They dinna know how hard I tried to do that. It got so I found 'twas impossible to be in the house, trapped with how he treated me. Then I heard Mrs. Bain talking to a bunch of ladies. Mrs. Bain, her being Mama's best friend and all." Eva gulped back tears. "She said, 'I promised not to say anything while Mr. MacDonald was alive, but my promise died with him. That girl is not MacDonald's offspring, if ya get my meaning. Her mother was with child when they married.'" Several of the women said they also knew and had always been wary of me because of it. They'd not spoken aloud about it for fear of angering my father and out of respect for Mama." It explained so many things. Why people acted like she'd done something wrong. Why her father pushed her away.

She wiped away tears that ran down her cheeks and dripped from her jaw. "Now ya will push me away." She sat up, intending to escape his arm before he could put any distance between them.

He ignored her attempt to get away and pulled her to his chest. "Eva, my poor Eva. Why would anyone blame you for what happened to your mother?"

"I am the fruit of sin." The words were garbled by tears. Perhaps he wouldn't understand them and be able to agree.

She needed to break free of his hold. Protect what was left of her heart. But instead, she clung to him and soaked his shirt with her tears as pain washed through her. Years of rejection, years of hopelessly longing for love from the man she thought was her father. The only father she'd ever known. Her life had been void of love from the day her mother died.

Until she married Pete. Not that love was spoken. Or even necessary. She felt it in the depths of her heart. This was where she wanted to belong, be accepted.

But she couldn't change the circumstances of her birth.

Nor would others be willing to overlook it. She'd learned that thoroughly.

She forced herself away from his embrace and put several inches between them as her heart beat one agonized throb after another.

She would stay, fulfill her vows, but she knew better than to expect the welcome she longed for and had enjoyed for the space of a few days.

11

Pete could not get a word past the anger raging inside his chest. What kind of people treated a sweet, innocent woman or child that way? What kind of man rejected a child that was born and grew up in his home?

He knew the answers. Had seen it so many times while living in the orphanage.

But he had to find a response for her pain. *God, You love her. Have always loved her. Please give me words to comfort her.*

He choked back his anger and pulled her back to his chest, ignoring the resistance she put up. He understood how hard it was to allow herself to hope for love and acceptance.

Finally, she gave in, though her arms curled between them, a protective barrier.

"Eva, you are not a product of sin. You are a

product of God's love. He formed you in your mother's womb. You are fearfully and wonderfully made. It says that in the Good Book. It also says God loves us with an everlasting love. To me, that means He loved us from before time and will into eternity and beyond."

Eva drew in a shuddering breath. But some of the stiffness left her body.

He continued. "I believe God brought you to me. You and I need each other." They both had deep hurts. Those wounds cried out one to the other. Together they could put the past to rest.

"Our promise to each other binds us. But it is our hearts that have found comfort and encouragement. Or perhaps I speak only for myself." The thought that she didn't feel the same caught at his breath and made it impossible to put air into his lungs.

"No, I feel it too." She moved one hand and pressed her palm to his chest right over his heart. "My heart cries out to yours. And I feel like yours answers with calm assurance. I believe God has brought us together."

Did he detect a hesitant note in her tone? "Are you regretting our decision?"

"Och, no. I have promised and I will gladly do. 'Tis enough."

'Tis enough? As if she wanted more. But he would not ask if that was so. He didn't want to take the chance she wanted things he couldn't give.

She eased back. "I'm sorry for crying on your shoulder and telling secrets ya didn't need to know."

He kept his arms around her, preventing her from escaping. "Don't be sorry. It helps me understand you better."

She lifted her eyes, full of caution and longing that made her irises hold more than one color of blue. "Aye? What do ya understand?"

He might have chuckled and made some off-hand remark if her tone had been teasing, but it wasn't. He heard the aching need for approval as clearly as if it had been stamped out in large letters on her forehead.

"Eva, I understand how lonely you must have been. How you must have ached for family and love.

She nodded, her eyes liquid with unshed tears.

Her sadness filled him, erasing caution. He pulled her forward and claimed her lips in a kiss. This one was unlike previous ones. He offered comfort. And commitment and a future.

A future that had certain limitations, but he hoped her willingness for kisses meant that perhaps, at some point, she'd be willing to renegotiate the terms of their agreement.

In the meantime, he meant to give her the acceptance she needed so badly.

She sighed in his arms and the last of her resistance evaporated.

He might have stayed there the rest of the day, but

she shifted. She was either restless or uncomfortable or both.

"Let's see if there are any more fish out there." He rose and pulled her to her feet.

They returned to the fishing rods. But she seemed distracted and after a few minutes, he took the rods. The sun was high overhead. "I'm hungry. How about you?"

"Starved to a shadow," she said.

"I'm going to build a fire and we'll fry fish for our dinner." Scotty had sent some bread rolls and dill pickles, which were the perfect accompaniment to fish.

"I'll clean the fish while ya build the fire." She held out a hand for his knife and knelt down, deftly scaling the fish. "I've been cleaning fish since I was knee-high to a tadpole."

He chuckled at the picture her words presented and set about preparing a fire. He glanced often at Eva as he worked. The tip of her tongue touched her upper lip as she concentrated. The fire burned and Pete sat back on his heels to watch her. She seemed so intent. So focused. So far away from him. And he didn't mean the distance between where he sat and where she knelt on the grass.

She looked up and met his gaze. She jerked her attention back to the fish, finished the task and brought the fillets to him.

Together, they fried the fish. He put a portion on

plates for each of them and they sat back. She didn't seem inclined to talk and he couldn't think what to say, so they worked in silence. An uncomfortable, pregnant silence.

She took a bite of the fish. "'Tis good. Thanks."

"Thanks to you for catching them and cleaning them."

"Aye." She ate a few more mouthfuls then paused. "Ya must think I'm plumb daft to be so upset about learning I'm a…" She waved her hands as if unable to speak a word describing the details of her birth.

Not that he could help her. Every word he knew was insulting, degrading.

"A sweet redhead," he supplied helpfully.

She laughed. "I'd like to think so." Her mouth flattened. She ate two more bites of fish and followed it with a bit of her bun. "I 'spect you've had worse things in yer life. Growing up in an orphanage and all. Hearing comments about the color of your skin." She gave him a bold look, her gaze going up and down his length.

He waited, wondering what she would say about her observations.

"You are colored by the sun. A strong and mighty man."

He grinned at her. "I'd like to think so." He echoed her own words. "But pain is pain no matter how or where we receive it."

"Aye. What was the worst thing about living in the orphanage?"

Memories flooded back, threatening to drown him in misery. "The worst thing about the orphanage was we didn't matter to anyone. I guess that's why—" Did he want to tell her everything? But then she'd laid her worst secret before him, trusting him to care. He could hardly do less.

"There was no time for coddling as it was called. You get hurt. You forget about it and move on. You're sad. Well, too bad. Sick? Take a dose of Epsom salts and hope for the best. We thought those who were taken in by a family had escaped the worst. But I discovered people can be cruel and uncaring wherever you go."

"Ya've experienced for yourself."

It wasn't a question, but an observation. He didn't wait for her to ask him to tell her. Suddenly, the details of his experiences flooded to his tongue.

"I was eleven years old when a family took me. I thought they were going to adopt me. They had four little girls. The father needed help with chores. I took care of the pigs, fed the chickens, weeded the garden, and a hundred other little things. I did it eagerly, out of gratitude. Oft times the family would be finished with the meal before I was done with a chore, but I didn't mind. I had a bed in the attic. A pallet really. But I didn't mind."

There must have been something in his voice that said otherwise to Eva, for she pressed to his side.

He continued. "Then the last potato was dug and put in the cellar. I thought now I would share meals with the family. Sit around the fire with the little girls and their parents." He swallowed hard, struggling to contain the echoing feeling of that experience. "Instead, the father gathered up my things and said they were done with me."

"I said, 'You don't want to keep me?' He shook his head and said, 'Get in the wagon.' No one said goodbye. Not even thank you. Instead, I was returned to the orphanage."

"Och, Pete. People can be so cruel." She bent her head to his shoulder. "Please tell me there were good things. Otherwise I might weep forever at how ya was treated."

"Wish I could. I soon learned that I was good for work, nothing else. People would take me for a season and then back I'd go. Until Maude, of course." His whole insides softened to know he belonged here. At the Circle A and with Eva.

"'Tis a sad life. How did ya come to be at the orphanage?"

He knew what she meant. "I was left as a baby. I have no idea who my parents are, so in some way I am like you."

"I at least had a home and when my mama was alive, I knew love. Sounds like ya never did."

"But I did. Once."

She shifted to look into his face. "Aye?"

"Yes, I was adopted."

"Ya have parents and a home?"

"I once did."

"Tell me what happened."

"I don't know where to begin."

"The beginning is always a good place."

He grinned at her. "I guess that's true." He let his thoughts go back, past the pain and scars to his earlier memory. "I only vaguely remembered living in the institution. I was maybe three when the Blakes took me in and adopted me. I guess I figured it was forever. A child takes so many things for granted." His life had seemed secure at that time. "What three-year-old gives any thought to the future? But things happen. Things no one has control over."

The memory of how his world had been shaken shot arrows through his heart.

"First, my papa died. We had to move. Mama said we would be all right. We'd find a place to live. For a time, we lived with a friend of hers, but then we had to leave. I don't know why. We slept in a woodshed behind the church. Mama said we'd be all right. But it was cold in the shed and we didn't have any food."

He didn't realize that his hands had corded into fists until Eva took them, uncurled his fingers, and pressed her hands to his flattened palms. He stared at their joined hands. Like a connection between his past and the present.

"Someone told Mama of the need for a housekeeper, so we walked a long way to a farm. I complained about how hungry I was. Mama said it would soon be over. But it wasn't. The farmer looked at Mama and at me and shook his head. 'Not with a child like him.'" His chest had turned to brick, making it impossible to breathe.

Eva pressed to his side. "Och, how awful. Did they at least give ya something to eat?"

"No." His answer was one hard syllable. "When we made our way back down the road I asked Mama what he meant. What was wrong with me? She hugged me and said nothing. I was made by God and that was enough for her and should be enough for everyone."

"'Tisn't always."

Pete nodded, though he wasn't sure she could see him do so.

"Tell me what happened next." Eva shuddered. "Though I am thinking it is a sad tale."

He wanted to roll his shoulders to ease the tension. Her head pressed to one side and not wanting her to move away, he settled for tipping his head back and forth.

"We ate berries we found along the road. Mama begged for food at a place. We kept moving. But we went slower and slower. I stole food from gardens and porches. Mama must have known, but she didn't say anything. I tried to keep her warm. She coughed a lot. Then one day she couldn't go on. She was too weak. She said we'd rest a bit, then continue our journey."

He should have known what to expect, but he was a child of five who believed a parent would take care of him.

"I asked where we were going. She said she was trusting God to provide an answer. The next day we arrived at this big building with a barn behind it and children peering out the window. I knew what it was. I remembered. It was the orphanage." He shuddered. Wished the story ended there. Wished he didn't need to continue, but Eva deserved to know it all. Besides, having started, he couldn't seem to stop reliving his past. Maybe he didn't even want to.

"I didn't protest as she led me to the door. Before she knocked, she hugged me. 'Petey, I don't want to do this, but I don't want to see you starve to death either. At least you'll be safe and fed here.' It took a moment for the truth of the words to sink in.

'You're leaving me here?' She nodded.

I asked when she was coming back. She shook her head and said she would if she could. I watched and waited for days. Until the matron told me my mother had died. That's when I knew nothing is forever."

His insides felt raw.

Eva wrapped her arms around him and held him tight. "Poor wee Pete. But dinna forget what ya told me. God loves ya from before time and into unending time."

He held her close. It was easy to believe that truth when her arms tightened around his waist.

"Aye and hasn't the Good Lord brought us together because He knows we understand how painful the past can be?"

He circled his arms around her and pressed his cheek to her head. They clung to each other. Their breathing synchronized. Warmth flowed from her to his heart and proved a balm to the old wounds. The barriers he'd constructed might have shrunk to knee height.

"Her name was Isabelle." Now, where had that memory come from? From the depths of his heart, behind those once-solid barriers. Cracks had formed in the thick concrete and a refreshing breeze wafted through.

EVA TIPPED her head back so she could look into Pete's face. "Do ya mean yer adoptive mother?"

"Yes. I didn't even know I knew her name." His eyes were warm.

She realized something that perhaps he didn't. "How long were you with the Blakes?"

He blinked. "I don't know for sure, but I suppose a couple of years."

"Aye, so for two years you had the love of a father and mother. 'Tis a God-given gift. And now ya belong in a family with John and Maude. I'd venture to say ya are blessed."

"You forgot something."

"Aye?"

"And now I have a wife to hold me."

He didn't say a wife to love or to love him. She would have said the words for him, but she feared a word spoken in haste would shatter the moment.

"Ya are blessed."

"And you?"

She grinned at him. "I am blessed too. A husband and a home." And if she wanted more 'twas her own burden to bear. She shifted so they sat side by side, an arm around the other.

The used dishes remained nearby. The sack of food that she thought might offer more cookies lay just beyond reach. Neither she nor Pete seemed inclined to leave their position.

The sun journeyed to the west and still, they sat, content to be together. Wrapped in warmth and understanding. If only they didn't have to move.

Tomorrow life for her would change greatly. "This is our last day together," she said.

His arm tightened around her shoulders. "I like to think that today is the first day of many. There will be plenty of times when we can be alone. Plus, we will have our evenings together. This, my dear wife, is the first day of the rest of our lives."

"Och, what a lovely thought."

He reached for the food sack and drew out cookies. He handed her two.

She bit into one, seeking a way to prolong the feeling of contentment. "I'm glad I told ya about my father. Now ya know everything about me."

He chuckled, his chest vibrating against hers. "I don't even know your favorite color. What is it?"

"Blue. No green. No purple." She laughed. "I just realized I don't have a favorite. Is that strange?"

"I don't think so. Just means a lot of things make you happy."

"Aye. What a kind thing to say. What's yer favorite color?"

He shifted and caught her braid and held it up. "This is. This color of red."

"Och, but how that warms my heart."

He grinned, his eyes brimming with approval that did indeed warm her heart. "What's your favorite food?"

Again she had to think. Then it hit her. "I find myself partial to anything Scotty makes. Pies, bread, pudding, cookies, potatoes…I could go on and on."

"I certainly agree with that."

"I hope he can teach me to be half as good as he is."

"I'm sure he can." There came a brief pause. Then he jerked as if something bit him.

She sat up and looked at him, her gaze running over his body. But she didn't see any ants or other troublesome insects. Her gaze stopped at his eyes.

"I just thought of something," he said.

"Aye?"

"It wasn't your red hair that people objected to. That was simply an easy scapegoat for their prejudice."

She stared at him. She'd never considered it. She took her braid and studied it. "Red hair is not a curse?"

He wrapped his hand around hers, the braid caught inside their grasp. "I'd certainly say otherwise."

She sat back, feeling rather pleased with her life. If only she could offer him something in return. Perhaps she could. "Pete, do ya think it isn't that all those others took you back to the orphanage that hurt so much as having Isabelle leave you?"

He considered her question a moment before he answered. "I guess that's so."

"Her leaving you had nothing to do with the color of your skin."

He didn't say anything. She wondered if he understood what she was trying to say.

Finally, he spoke. "I guess it doesn't matter to everyone."

"Aye, it doesn't matter to those who count."

He laughed, the sound soft and deep in his chest. "I believe you are right on that matter."

Silence again settled over them, accompanied by contentment.

A flock of ducks landed on the water of the quiet pond.

"Coming home to rest," Pete said. He sighed. "I suppose it means we should go home as well."

She didn't want to move, but he rose and pulled her to her feet.

They cleaned up the area, returned to the wagon, and headed home.

The next day was Sunday. Everyone would visit and meet her. Fear and excitement filled her. She reached for Pete's hand and he turned his palm to hers and smiled at her.

His words of acceptance would give her the courage she needed to face the others.

12

Eva squeezed her eyes closed. She dinna want to wake up. Dinna want to get out of bed. Dinna want to go downstairs and meet everyone.

Pete plopped his pillow to her head. "Come on, lazybones. I'm not going to let you hide out here all day. So get up and get dressed."

She squinted one eye open. "Could be I'm sick. All that fish yesterday, ya know."

He chuckled. "Seems I recall you saying you ate mostly fish back east."

"Aye, and don't I have a loose tongue?"

He grinned. "Get up, dear wife. I can't wait for the others to meet you."

"And I could delay it forever if I had my way."

"Don't be silly. They are going to love you and you are going to love them." He took her hands and pulled her from the bed. They stood toe to toe, she in her nightgown and he already fully clothed, making her feel vulnerable.

"Aye, I might as well get dressed now that I'm up." She slipped away to the other room. Then remembered she needed a dress and hurried back to get it, his chuckles accompanying her every step. She paused at the doorway to cast an exasperated look at him. "Ya are enjoying this far too much."

She closed the door against his laughter, hoping he wouldn't hear her chuckles as she washed, rebraided her hair, and rolled the braid around her head, pinning it into place. She'd chosen her pale blue dress because she felt most comfortable in it and knew she'd need to be at her best to meet everyone.

Her stomach did a nosedive and she caught the edges of the washstand and told herself to be calm. The sooner she got this over with the better for her nerves.

Pete waited for her outside the door and they descended the stairs together. He'd already been down to assist John and the older couple were in the kitchen.

She took her usual place at the table. Tomorrow she would begin to assist Scotty. Today, quelling the rising and falling of her stomach required all her energy. She took small portions of the food as it was passed but wondered if she'd be able to swallow a single bite.

She'd choked back three mouthfuls when the sound of horses approaching tightened her throat. She put aside her fork, knowing she wouldn't be able to force anything more down. She pressed her hands to her knees.

Pete covered her hands with one of his. "They'll tend the horses then come to the house."

She tried to fill her lungs, but they'd turned to stone.

A few minutes later, boot steps echoed on the veranda and the door burst open. Four men came in with much noise. They saw her and every sound ended.

"Boys, shut the door. Were ye born in a barn?" Scotty said.

Pete stood, one hand resting on Eva's shoulder. "Boys, I'd like you to meet my wife."

She could hear at least one of them gulp.

Two of the men before her looked enough alike to be the brothers, Noah and Adam. Both blond and blue-eyed. The third had an eager look about him that made her think he was Sam. Also blond. The last had to be Mike. Pete had failed to say he had unusual silvery-blue eyes.

Sam was the first to regain his senses and hurried forward. "Pleased to meet you. I'm Sam."

The others joined him and Pete introduced everyone. They were all kind in their welcome but didn't completely fail to hide their surprise and curiosity. Thankfully, none of them asked the questions that must be filling their thoughts, but she knew Pete would be dealing with them later. She could almost feel sorry for him, but she knew he didn't need her concern. He was well able to take care of himself.

The four of them greeted John and Maude. Said the herd was well and content in a draw filled with grass, then they hurried away to join their wives.

Her lungs released in a whoosh that everyone could hear.

Pete chuckled as he again sat next to her. "See, they're harmless as kittens."

Scotty gave a wheezing laugh. "Does me good ta see them so surprised."

Eva managed to swallow the last of her breakfast. The worst was yet to come. Meeting the women. In one curious crowd. She was glad she was done eating because her throat closed off enough to threaten to choke her.

Maude gathered up the used dishes and carried them to the dishpan.

Eva pushed her chair back, intending to offer to help, but Pete caught her hand. "Not today," he murmured, and she settled back again.

The aroma of cooking meat filled the room. Huge pots sat on the work table. She guessed they were vegetables ready to cook. As Scotty took something into the pantry, she saw an array of pies.

He'd been busy yesterday and probably Maude as well. She'd be helping next time.

Pete carried chairs to the veranda and arranged them for the church service.

John took his Bible, rolled out to the veranda, and took a spot facing the grouped chairs.

Eva didn't wait for Pete to choose a place for them. She went to the back corner and sat. If she were to follow her heart, she'd pull the chair around the corner and out of sight.

No. She wou'nae. She was proud to be Pete's wife and would meet the others with the same grace she'd seen in her mother. *Thank ya, Ma for being a sweet woman despite the shame and disgrace ya lived with.* For the first time since she'd learned the news about her father, she was grateful that he'd at least treated Eva's mother kindly.

The sound of voices drew her attention to the path to the cabins. They were all coming at once. A crowd of them.

Pete moved to her side and rested his hand on her shoulder. "You'll soon see for yourself that they'll welcome you."

Ten adults, a babe in arms, and five children came toward her. They clambered to the veranda and stopped, waiting for Pete to make the introductions.

He pulled Eva to her feet. "Everyone, this is my wife, the beautiful Eva."

Aye, dinna that make her feel ready to meet man or beast?

Beginning on his left, he introduced each one.

Noah was married to Lainie and they were raising her brother, Boyd, and sister, Missy. Eva remembered Lainie had squatted on Circle A land. Good thing he had told her about the others. It made it easier for her to place them in her mind.

Adam had married Grace, Sam's sister, if Eva remembered correctly. They had no children at their side.

Eva let out a barely-there sigh. At least she was'nae the only woman without bairns.

Next to them was Mike with those startling silvery eyes. He'd married Beth. Eva tried to recall what Pete had told her about the couple. Dinna he say that Mike had been left at the orphanage by his sister who, instead, married Beth's father and helped raise her?

Eva smiled, knowing everyone would take it as an acknowledgment of the greeting each one gave her, but more than that, it was amusement to think how God had brought Mike and Beth together. Between them was Dakota, whom they'd brought from the orphanage. The same orphanage where Pete had spent most of his life.

Sam's friendly face caused Eva's smile to widen. He'd married Yvette.

Remembering the story Pete had told about how they'd been kidnapped because Yvette's father was rich had led them to the two boys they now were raising. Tad and Gil.

"There. You've met everyone now," Pete said. He

leaned close and murmured close to her ear. "And survived."

She tipped her chin. "Aye, I dinna think otherwise."

At the same time, Mike leaned forward to give Pete a playful punch on his shoulder. "What kind of stories have you told her about us?"

John cleared his throat. "If you'd all find a seat…"

There was much shuffling and rearranging of chairs until everyone settled into place.

Maude held an autoharp and began to strum it.

Eva recognized the tune to *Amazing Grace* and dinna she hear in her head the tune played on the bagpipes.

When Maude began to sing, the others joined her. A mixture of deep voices and high children's with everything in between.

Eva closed her eyes and let the music soar through her heart. She opened her mouth and joined her voice to the others.

Tears pushed against her eyelids, but she held them back. 'Twas foolish to wear her emotions so close to the surface.

They sang another hymn then John opened his Bible. "Today we are so blessed. Maude and I never dreamed we'd have this much family to share our lives with. Now that all of you are married, Maude can stop trying to find wives for our boys."

Eva's head came up. Maude had been trying to find wives for the men? Had she picked out someone for Pete? A stab of jealousy pierced her heart. She pushed it away. He'd married her. And they'd promised to stay together. She dinna worry that his heart belonged elsewhere and she focused her attention back on John.

He smiled tenderly at his wife. "God has provided. That reminds me of Abraham. In Genesis chapter twenty-two, he took Isaac up the mount to give as a sacrifice. He knew he could trust God and his faith was not in vain. God provided a ram to take Isaac's place." John looked around the assembly. "God is the same as He was back there. Able to provide for our every need. Let's trust Him."

He closed in prayer.

Eva kept her gaze down after the 'Amen.' John's words had comforted and challenged her. The life she'd chosen might require a sacrifice of her dream for a large family. Children, she meant, not all these people surrounding her. But God would provide the grace she needed.

Chairs were shuffled around so the adults formed a circle. The children moved away. Dakota and Gil played with a pair of dogs. Missy and Tad played some sort of game under the nearby tree. As far as Eva could tell, the game involved arranging twigs and yellow leaves. Boyd remained with the adults.

Yvette leaned forward. "How did you two meet?"

Eva chuckled. "By accident." She felt the expectant waiting of the others. "Aye." She wasn't prepared to say anything more, nor did Pete jump in with an explanation.

Baby Neil fussed. Dillon took him, but he wouldn't settle. Dillon sat next to Pete and handed the baby to him. "See if he'll quiet for you."

Eva watched Pete with the baby. He held him like he'd done it a hundred times.

An ache the size of the rolling hills squeezed every other thought from her heart. Wou'nae he make a good father?

The baby stopped crying and soon fell asleep.

Eva kept her gaze on the baby, although she felt all eyes on her. Seems they weren't about to forget that she hadn't given an explanation as to how they'd met.

Pete must have guessed the same thing, for he said, "Eva is from down east. Pictou, Nova Scotia. It's on the ocean, but she says the wide prairies are better than looking at the sea. Says she can see even farther."

"Aye," she said. "I feel like I can see forever."

No one laughed or even chuckled.

She could feel their consideration. They had questions but understood neither Pete nor Eva were ready to answer them.

Sam looked toward the pile of lumber. "Dillon says you brought Eva back with you when you returned from the fort." Silence followed his statement.

Eva understood it was to give one of them a chance to offer more information.

Pete handed the sleeping baby to Abby. "Come on,

I'll show you the lumber." He strode from the veranda and then paused, looking over his shoulder in silent impatience.

"I'd like to talk about the project," John said and rolled down the ramp to Pete's side.

The men rose and followed.

Eva got to her feet too. She'd go with them. Better to talk about boards and nails than to face an inquisition from the women. But Yvette said, "Eva, let the men enjoy their discussion."

Eva sat down, knowing her cheeks would be as red as her hair. She hadn't known women weren't welcome. She braced herself for the questions.

But Yvette again filled the silence. "I want to make some pickles, but I don't know how."

Scotty had gone inside, so he wasn't there to offer his ideas.

"I could use some help too," Lainie said. "The last batch I made is too vinegary." She tipped her head back to look in the screen door and raised her voice. "Do you think Scotty could give us a lesson?"

Scotty came to the door. "What are ya wantin' poor old Scotty fer?"

Lainie and Yvette took turns talking as they explained.

"I'll do it. How about Tuesday mornin'? The whole works of ye. I'm guessin' ya could all use a reminder."

The women all agreed that suited them.

Tuesday morning. Eva closed her eyes and slowed

her breathing. Could she possibly find an excuse to be away? Except, she needed to learn everything she could from Scotty.

"I'm going to rest." Maude went inside.

The conversation turned to stories about pickles and gardening and Eva began to relax.

Perhaps a bit too soon.

"Do you think Maude is disappointed none of the men took her advice to marry the mail-order brides she had chosen for them?" Beth said.

"Especially when she went to so much work to select what she thought was the right one for each of the men," Grace added. Her smile said she held no resentment toward Maude for her efforts.

If Grace and the others were satisfied with how things had turned out for them, so was Eva and she dismissed the twist of jealousy.

"I was the only one to have Maude's chosen bride show up demanding Noah marry her." Lainie chuckled but shook her head at the same time.

Eva looked at each speaker. Had Maude chosen a bride for Pete? No. Wou'nae he have said so? Ha'nae they shared their deepest secrets yesterday? She leaned back again.

But then realized the women were all looking at her. Was it her hair? Or their curiosity?

She swallowed hard. "'Twas a nice service, was'nae it?"

Yvette nodded. "We love these simple gatherings."

"Tell us about Nova Scotia. Are your folks still there?" Lainie said.

"Och, no. My parents are both dead, God rest their souls."

The others murmured condolences.

She turned to where the men gathered at the stack of lumber. The canvas covering had been thrown back. Men waved their arms and pointed. She chuckled. "Looks like they see the completed building."

The women were distracted.

"My two aren't eager for the school to be constructed," Yvette said. "They'd far sooner follow Sam around all day long." She sighed expansively. "Though I can't blame them. I'd do the same if I didn't have to take care of the house."

"Missy is eager to go to school but not Boyd," Lainie said. "I confess I'll miss them, even if it's only for a few hours a day."

Beth nodded. "Dakota says school is a waste of time. I hope whoever we get for a teacher is prepared to make learning fun."

"We should make a list of things we'd like to see for a school teacher," Lainie said and the three with school-age children bent their heads together.

Abby listened, even though it would be years before Neil would need schooling.

Grace got to her feet. "Eva, would you like to accompany me? I'll show you my home."

Eva didn't hesitate. This talk of children burned at her insides.

The two of them went down the path. Grace waved at Adam. Pete looked up, saw Eva, and lifted a hand as far as his waist. Not really a wave and yet she felt a connection across the distance. She lifted her hand in a similar fashion as she walked on with Grace. They went to the cabin second from the end in the line of buildings. 'Twas almost like a street in town, Eva thought. The yards adjoined. Each house had plants in front. A few late blossoms colored the foliage.

Grace opened the door and ushered her in.

Eva looked around. It was small but as neat as a pin. "'Tis very cozy. Not unlike the house I grew up in." She chuckled. "Except tidier. My father was a collector. After Mama died, his collections kinda took over."

"I'm sorry about your parents. It's hard to be an orphan, but I've seen how it can be used by God to build strong men and women."

"Is Adam an orphan?"

"No, his mother remarried after his father died and the stepfather didn't care to have two half-grown boys hanging about. No, I was meaning Pete. And Sam too, of course. But I'm sure you already know that."

"Aye." What other reply could she give?

"This is the kitchen and dining area."

"'Tis very nice." A shining stove, a pretty rug, neat cupboards with some pretty dishes displayed on an open shelf. The table had a large white doily in its center with a vase holding a collection of colorful leaves and branches. Eva blinked hard. She would not cry. Would not admit that she wanted children and a home like this.

Grace showed her the sitting area with two matching armchairs and a small settee. Beside it, a bookcase with a handful of books.

Then Grace pointed out the two bedrooms. "One for us and one for our children." She hugged her arms across her chest. "I hope we have some soon."

That announcement made Eva feel even lonelier. She admired the quilt on the bed and the pictures on the wall, then Grace invited her to have tea.

Eva glanced out the window and saw the men were still at the pile of lumber, discussing wildly. "'Twould be nice." Better than returning to the others and their curiosity and talk of children.

A few minutes later, Grace set two pretty teacups on the table and sat across from Eva.

Pa had drunk his tea out of the saucer, but Eva knew it 'twas considered rude by most. She sipped the hot liquid from the cup. The tea was good and she began to relax.

"This reminds me of when my mother was alive," she said. "Dinna she like her cup of tea every afternoon?"

"My mother did as well."

Eva looked up startled. "But aren't you Sam's

sister? I thought—" She was certain Sam was a true orphan.

Grace's smile was gentle. "I was adopted. He wasn't. He left to make sure I was." Her voice caught. "I had a good life because of what he did."

Eva realized it would take her time to figure out all the connections and learn the stories that brought each of them to this place. Perhaps someday, she'd add her story.

"Of course, he had a good life too but only because Maude and John gave him one. Though I guess it would be more correct to say God had His hand on what happened." She grew thoughtful. "I expect the same could be said of you and Pete."

"Aye, I would say so for sure." But she offered nothing more.

Grace gave her a gentle smile again. "When you're ready, I'd love to hear the details of how you and Pete met, but until then I won't probe."

"Aye." But what about the others?

Grace must have read her thoughts. "I think the others will give you time as well."

Eva didn't point out that Grace dinna sound wholly convinced.

"Pete, what do you think?"

He'd been staring at Grace and Adam's home and hadn't heard what John said. "Sounds good to me."

John chuckled. "Maybe I suggested you should go to the far north of the ranch and stay there until freeze up."

That got Pete's complete attention. "Did you?"

The others laughed.

John shook his head. "I said we could get the shell up in one day if we had enough help. I think I'll speak to Abner about it." He looked down the road. "I thought he and Ilsa might have been here today."

Pete looked in the direction of town. It was the first time the couple hadn't been there in a long while.

"I hope everything is all right," John said, then returned his attention to the pile of lumber.

Just as quickly, Pete's gaze went back to the cabin. At least Eva was with Grace, who might not be as demanding in her questions as some of the others. Though why was he concerned? He and Eva understood each other. And if she wanted to reveal how they'd met, that was up to her.

He wouldn't be telling anyone unless she did. He smiled. That was their secret. As were the terms of their marriage.

His smile flattened. He hoped she would be agreeable to changing their agreement in the near future. Every day he grew more eager to make her truly his wife.

John decided he was ready to go back to the house and Pete cast one more look at the cabin where Eva was and then helped John across the yard and up the ramp.

"Bout time," Scotty said. "The meal's getting cold." He banged the metal triangle to call everyone in for the noon meal they all shared. Their Sunday tradition.

John wheeled inside. The women and children trooped indoors. The men hurried back from the lumber pile.

Pete hung back. Finally, Grace and Eva left the house across the yard and came in his direction. He studied Eva's expression. She looked calm. As she drew near, she smiled and his insides lost a knot he wasn't aware was there.

He crooked his elbow toward her and she took it as they joined the others.

Her hand tightened as she took in the extended table and the people crowding around it. With him and Eva, there were twenty people. And little Neil who'd been put down on the cot.

"'Tis a large family," she murmured.

"Your dream come true."

"Aye." She sounded disappointed, rather than pleased, then smiled up at him, her eyes flashing with something he couldn't name. "I have ya ta thank for this."

Before he could reply, John waved them toward a pair of chairs.

They joined the others around the table.

"Shall we sing the doxology as grace?" John said and began, "'Praise God from whom all blessings flow…'"

Beside Pete, Eva joined in the singing. Under the table, he squeezed her hand and hoped she would know he counted her as one of his blessings. Perhaps his greatest.

"Amen," they sang in harmony.

"God is good," John said.

"All the time," they echoed in unison.

"All the time," John said.

"God is good," the refrain echoed around the table.

His heart full of gratitude, Pete took from the serving dishes as they were passed around.

God had blessed him so greatly he would not pine after the things he didn't have.

A marriage in name only was enough for him. Knowing Eva and having her at his side, smiling and laughing, was sufficient. More than he'd ever dared hope for.

13

The next morning, Eva dressed hurriedly and rushed downstairs while Pete was still yawning and stretching. Today, she would begin to fulfill her agreement to help Scotty and Maude.

Scotty greeted her with a cup of tea.

"Ya dinna have to bother."

"No bother, missy. If tea is yer drink, then I'll make tea."

She gulped a few swallows. "Now tell me what to do. I'm here ta work, ya know."

He waggled his eyebrows. "Eh, I thought you was here to make Pete happy. Happy looks good on him."

She turned away, hoping he wou'nae notice the heat rushing up her cheeks that would paint them to match her hair. Knew she hadn't turned soon enough when Scotty cackled.

"Looks good on you too."

"What do you want me to do?" she asked, hoping he would leave the subject.

"Ya can fry these." He handed her a bowl of cooked potatoes. She set a large frying pan to heat, added a dollop of drippings, and sliced the potatoes into the sizzling fat.

Scotty nodded approval.

She turned the pork that was frying. And when she heard Pete go into John and Maude's bedroom, she took the pork out and broke eggs into the pan.

"Looks to me like I can lay abed in the mornin's," Scotty said, his voice revealing approval.

"There is so much I need ya to teach me." Seeing his disbelief, she added. "I never could make decent bread and my pies dinna pass approval."

"I'll teach ya and with pleasure."

She smiled at him. He smiled back and she felt like she'd passed some sort of test with flyin' colors.

"And coffee. I'll need to learn how to make that."

She insisted Scotty sit while she took the food to the table and then the five of them sat around the much smaller table. The extra boards had been removed and stored in a closet in the hall.

"Good meal," Pete said.

The others thanked her.

She didn't want to take all the credit. "Scotty is a good teacher."

He cleared his throat. "There was nothin' to teach ya."

After breakfast, she helped clean up the kitchen.

Maude had set up washtubs outside and scrubbed clothes. Eva helped rinse them and hang them on the line, then returned to the kitchen and helped Scotty prepared the noon meal. Following his instructions, she made a rhubarb pudding.

She enjoyed learning how to cook like Scotty did and she liked his company, but several times she forgot where she was as she stared out the window hoping for a glimpse of Pete.

Scotty chuckled. "He'll be back come dinnertime. Never knew a one of them to miss a meal." He sighed. "Kind of miss feedin' them all. Missy, truth is, there ain't enough work cooking for four or five people. Exceptin' for Sunday dinner, ya know."

She jerked from the window. Sounded like she might have to prove she was needed.

"Now don't get me wrong," Scotty continued. "I'm more than grateful for yer help. Might take me out to the hills for a few days."

Eva set about preparing carrots to bake. It was a recipe she'd learned from her mother and was glad to show Scotty something new.

By the time the sun was high overhead, the laundry flapped in the wind, a delicious meal was ready and Eva was hungry. She wasn't about to admit it, but that was the hardest she'd ever worked.

The afternoon was not as busy. Scotty bemoaned the

fact that without all the boys to eat his offerings, they had only to prepare leftovers for the evening meal. Eva brought in the laundry as it dried and ironed what needed it. Some she only folded into piles to be put away.

Scotty had gone to his cabin. Maude and John had gone to their sitting room. Pete was doing something outside. She'd heard mention of a fence that needed repairing. She had the kitchen to herself and her thoughts.

And dinna they go down unbidden trails?

Preparing meals and helping in the house was satisfying. Only it was John and Maude's house and how she ached for her own. And dinna Scotty's comments make her think she was'nae truly needed?

'Nough feelin' sorry for meself. Ha'nae Ma taught her to count her blessin's? Having learned the truth about her mother, she realized it cou'nae have always been easy for her, and yet dinna she smile and appear calm about life?

Could Eva do less?

She had a husband who was kind and handsome. She had a home full of friendliness. A good teacher in Scotty. She glanced out the window, saw Abby taking little squares of white flannel from the line. Diapers for wee Neil. A lump blocked Eva's throat. But never mind. She could enjoy the other children. In fact, she'd make cookies for the older ones and she turned to the task.

When they were baked, she took some outside to the children.

After supper, Pete suggested they go for a walk.

Eva's flagging energy renewed. "Aye, I'd like that."

They walked up the hill to the bench and sat. "Tell me about your day," she said.

He did and then asked the same of her.

He took her hand. "I'm glad you're finding life here to your liking."

"What's not to like?" She rested her head on his shoulder. Being with him pushed away all the silly longings she'd had earlier. His gentle good night kiss drove away any hint of wishing for more.

Scotty hustled about after dinner the next day preparing for the pickle making. Eva was less enthused. Having all the young women in the house, made her heart skip like a frightened cat. Wou'nae they press her for information? She loathed to confess how Pete had rescued her from her dire situation. Dinna it sound like he'd married her out of pity? But then, maybe he had.

She smiled to herself. Pity or no, she was blessed to have been rescued. And faithful to her promises she would be. Aye, she might have silly longings from time to time, but they'd only last a moment. All she had to do was think of walking and talking with Pete, holding his hand, and sharing gentle kisses to make her admit she had more than enough to be glad about.

Scotty set out jars, vinegar and a number of other ingredients. "Come with me to get the picklin' vegetables."

She followed him to the garden.

"I'm goin' ta make a pickle recipe I got from an old codger who taught me ta cook. It was on a ranch down in Montana territory. I was his helper, ya see. He called it the end-of-the-garden pickle. Said a person could use anything left in the garden. Carrots is always good." He pulled a dozen and put them in the basket. "Need enough for all of us." He pulled another dozen, then lifted blankets off some vines. "Good. Some late summer squash." He added what he could find.

They went up and down the rows.

Eva picked late green beans to add to the mix. There were onions still in the ground and she pulled the smaller ones to pickle while Scotty put other vegetables in the basket.

"That'll do."

They returned to the kitchen just as the others entered.

Tension gripped Eva's insides. She'd enjoyed her visit with Grace, but today all the women were there. Pete had gone to stake out the site for the schoolhouse. Maude and John took Neil and sat on the verandah to supervise the children. She must face this situation alone. She squared her shoulders. Aye, and she could and would.

Scotty put the women to work preparing the vegetables. And dinna they talk as they worked? Not that she expected anything else.

They talked about cooking and housekeeping. She joined the laughter as Yvette told of a recent failure. "How was I to know that milk boiled over so fast?" She wrinkled her nose. "And smelled so bad cooking on the stovetop?"

Eva settled back, content and happy to listen to the stories.

Lainie paused from peeling carrots. "What's it like down east? Do you eat differently?"

Eva swallowed hard. "Aye, we eat a lot of fish." She hurried to add, "Pete and I ate fish t'other day. Caught it in the river." Remembered they called it a creek but didn't correct herself.

Scotty stood at the end of the table. "Youse got the vegetables ready?"

They finished up.

"Now listen to me," Scotty said. "There's some things ya ought to keep in mind when makin' pickles."

He had their attention as he explained how to prepare the jars, then had them put the vegetables into a pot big enough to cook half a dozen lobsters. They measured vinegar, sugar, and spices into the pot. As soon the mixture boiled, they added the vegetables.

A little later jars sat cooling on the cupboard and the women stood admiring them and thanking Scotty.

"I better get home and take care of supper and the children," Yvette said.

The others also departed, leaving Scotty and Eva alone in the kitchen.

She let out a deep sigh that emptied her lungs.

Scotty chuckled. "Was a bit of a trial, was it?"

Suddenly she laughed, surprised by a realization. "Och, no. 'Twas fun."

Still smiling, she helped Scotty set out the food for supper, all the while listening for the sound of Pete's return. Her heart leaped when she heard his boots on the veranda floor. It was all she could do not to rush to the door to greet him.

She might not have hidden her reaction as well as she thought for Scotty cackled with glee, but she ignored him as she watched for Pete to enter.

He stepped inside and scanned the room until he saw her. He smiled, something in his eyes saying how glad he was to see her.

No doubt, her eyes said the same thing.

She ducked her head, lest the others see how it pleasured her to see his welcome.

OVER THE NEXT FEW DAYS, Pete was happy to see how well Eva fit in. She had no trouble managing meals, even when Scotty disappeared into the west for a day. She made cookies for the children and spent a few hours entertaining them. Every evening Pete took Eva's hand and they walked. Sometimes to the bench. Sometimes up a hill to watch the sunset.

John and Maude had suggested he spend another week at the ranch, but he knew it couldn't continue. The other men deserved to spend time there, taking care of John and being with their wives and children.

He knew Eva was worried about being left.

"You won't be lonely," he assured her.

"Aye, but I will."

He pretended confusion. "How is that possible? There are enough people here it should be called a town."

Her smile seemed lopsided.

He caught her in his arms and smiled down at her upturned face. "Are you saying you'll miss me?"

She wrapped her arms around his waist and hugged him so tight he could hardly breathe. "Dinna tease me. Ya know I will miss ya."

He held her and bent his chin to her hair. "And I will miss you too."

"Not with all those cows for company."

He roared with laughter at her injured tone.

He meant to spend every minute with her he could before he must leave.

Sunday came all too soon. He would ride out that night.

He pulled his chair as close to hers as possible for the Sunday service and tried to concentrate on what John had to say. But the idea of leaving her hammered at his thoughts until he barely heard a word.

It was all he could do not to hold her hand every minute of the day, but she'd helped Scotty prepare the big meal and helped him serve it, not taking her place at his side until she had done so.

The others went their separate ways as soon as the meal was dispensed with. For the first time, Pete understood why the couples were so eager to rush away.

"Let's go for a walk," he said to Eva.

"I thought ya'd never ask." She took his hand and pressed close to him as they headed toward the bench.

But when they got there, neither of them seemed inclined to sit and they continued up the hill.

"I leave after supper," he said.

"Aye." The word came slowly, then she rushed on. "But dinna worry about me. I'll be fine. Just fine."

"I know you will be. But it won't keep me from thinking about you the whole time I'm gone."

"That will purely be a waste of time."

He stopped walking and pulled her to his chest. "I couldn't stop thinking of you even if I wanted to and I don't want to."

"'Tis good to know."

They sat on the grass, shoulders pressed together.

His heart was full but he couldn't find words to express his thoughts.

How could it be less than two weeks since they had met and married? He couldn't imagine life without her now. A shiver crossed his shoulders as he thought of something John said on occasion. Easy come. Easy go.

Surely it didn't apply to him and Eva. They'd made vows. He meant to keep his and trusted her to keep hers, but would being apart put their relationship to the test? Would she realize life went on without him? Would she get used to him not being in her life?

14

Eva had never known days to pass so slowly. She helped with laundry, did the ironing, assisted in preparing meals, but as Scotty said, with only four of them, their meals didn't take a lot of time.

She went to the garden every day searching for fresh vegetables.

Adam had stayed behind or she might have sought Grace out for company. But she didn't care to intrude. Even when Adam was at the site of the proposed schoolhouse and doing something by the barn, Grace was often at his side. And they often went riding together.

How Eva envied her.

For some reason, Eva didn't seek out any of the others. Aye, and dinna she know the reason. Pure ugly envy. She told herself she didn't feel the way she did, but her heart refused to listen.

Abby invited her to visit and she went there one afternoon. It was a pleasant way to spend a couple hours, but dinna Eva's insides burn with longing to have what Abby had? She soon slipped away.

Saturday finally came. She busied herself making pies under Scotty's supervision. She chased him away from the house in the afternoon.

"Go to your cabin and enjoy the balmy sunshine." After he left, she prepared potatoes and turnips for the next day's meal.

Everything was ready for the morrow. A stew simmered for the evening meal. John and Maude were comfortable visiting on the veranda.

Eva escaped upstairs to the room she shared with Pete. She ran her fingers across the top quilt on his bed. She'd washed the sheets. The bed was neat, ready and waiting for him…just as she was. Her heart would be content when he was back where she could see him, touch him, and steal a kiss or two.

She went to the window and looked out, recalling how she'd watched him that first day. And even then, dinna she know she'd found the place she wanted to be? The place her hungry heart had longed for all her life?

She rested her forehead on the frame for a moment. A movement below caught her eye. Tad and Gil playing a game.

Her heart lurched and she turned from the window.

She had Pete. He'd given her a home and family. 'Twas enough. She pressed her hand to her chest as if she could contain the ache. And acknowledged something. He'd claimed her heart. Every beat of it. 'Twas not part of their agreement but there it 'twas nevertheless. She loved him. He'd not given her his heart, but it dinna matter. He had taken hers.

Filled with restless energy, she pulled a rag from her pocket and began to dust. She did the top of the dresser, moving the rock, the child's book, and the locket. He'd told her about the rock and what it meant to him. A reminder of false hope, hadn't he said?

Pete, I will not be the cause of false hope in yer life.

She moved aside the broken locket. He'd never said, but she guessed it had belonged to his adoptive mother, Isabelle. Or reminded him of her. Poor little boy.

Was the child's book a reminder of a happy past? She closed her eyes as the longing for children again rose like a surging tide.

After a moment, she opened her eyes and put the book down. 'Twas enough to give her heart and affection wholly to Pete.

The dresser finished, she moved around the room. Stopped to stare at the spot where he'd asked if she would like to hang a picture. Och, how could she have forgotten? She rushed to her trunk and removed the sampler her mother had made. She'd find a nail and hang it over her bed.

Might as well dust inside the wardrobe. She opened the doors. A pair of rolled-up socks and a rumpled hanky were on the floor of the cupboard. She pulled them out. Behind them was a crumpled piece of paper. Odd. Pete was'nae a messy man. Might it be something important?

She smoothed the pages and read the words.

She read them a second time.

Dear Trudy, Now that we've gotten to know each other, I wish to ask you to marry me. Keep in mind, I don't know who my parents are, but one of them had swarthy skin. John says I might have Spaniard blood in me. Others say native or black.

There was a splotch of ink that ruined the page which explained why he had thrown it aside.

Eva sat back on her heels, her heart hammering in her ears.

He'd planned to marry another.

But then so had she, which he knew having witnessed her humiliation.

Why hadn't he told her?

Why keep it a secret? Unless he regretted this lost opportunity?

Had he offered to marry her out of pity?

She stuffed the paper in her pocket, threw the hankie and socks back inside the wardrobe and firmly closed the doors.

She tiptoed down the stairs and out the back door, releasing a quiet breath when she encountered no one.

She circled the garden and turned her steps the opposite way she and Pete usually went. Not wanting to get lost and disorientated, she walked around the buildings, staying at a distance, doing her best to be out of sight of anyone who might be able to see her.

Her heart bled as if gouged by a thousand fish hooks. The big kind.

She sank to the ground, rested her head on her upturned arms, and cried. She would have wailed like a banshee but feared someone might hear her. Tears burned down her cheeks.

After a time, she'd cried out all her tears. And she'd made up her mind.

She'd married Pete and promised it was forever. He'd made the same promise and she knew he would keep it. Aye, but ha'nae she hoped for more? A real marriage? A home and children? And most of all, love?

She needed to remember that rock on Pete's dresser. Fool's gold. False hope. False dreams.

The sun still shone. The wind still blew. The grass waved. Life went on.

With leaden feet and a heavy heart, she returned to the house. 'Twould soon be time to serve the evening meal.

Then she'd face another night alone, but this time without the eagerness and anticipation of Pete's soon return. The thought that he'd chosen another weighed in her heart like a giant boulder.

. . .

Her heart still hurt when she rose the next morning and went downstairs to make breakfast. She'd told Scotty not to come over until time to eat. Adam slipped in to help John. Eva smiled and bid him good morning. He hurried to the bedroom. As soon as John was up, Adam left and Scotty came.

She set out breakfast.

"Best put a plate out for Pete," Scotty said. "He'll be anxious for some good food." Scotty cackled. "And to see ya."

"Aye." Her smile felt frozen in place. She put on another plate and utensils.

At the sound of approaching riders, she jerked upright and stared at the door. Horses first, she reminded herself. And forced her feet to get the pot of coffee. She filled all the cups, including Pete's. Even her own, though she still didn't care for the strong brew.

Scotty chortled but choked off the sound quickly.

John and Maude exchanged knowing looks. No doubt they thought her distraction was due to anticipation of Pete's return.

Her nerves rattling, Eva turned back to the stove as if she'd forgotten something. Boots echoed across the wooden floor of the veranda. Many boots. She recalled they all greeted John and Maude before they went to their homes.

The door opened and five men burst through.

Eva stared at the group though she saw only one

man. Pete. He jerked his hat from his head, looked in her direction, and smiled. Aye and dinna his eyes say he was happy to see her? Or was she giving him her own thoughts?

She tried to smile. Couldn't make the corners of her mouth tip up.

His smile slid off his face. He quirked his eyebrows, questioning her.

The others went to John and Maude and Eva forced her attention in that direction.

After hurried greetings, the others left and Pete took his place at the table.

Eva looked around. Had she forgotten something? But no, everythin' was on the table and everyone waited for her.

She somehow forced her reluctant feet to take her to sit at Pete's side.

"Hi," he whispered.

She nodded.

Thankfully, John announced grace, and then they were busy passing around the food. John asked for a report on the cows. She heard Pete's answer, but the words blurred like the distant roll of the surf.

Somehow she made it through the meal. Pete rose, looked at her with uncertainty.

"I will clean the kitchen," she said, hurrying away with an armload of used dishes.

He grabbed something and followed. "I'll help."

Dinna her heart ache to enjoy his company? But

she cou'nae forget that letter. "Ya dinna need to," she managed on a croak. "Ya could go tell John about the cows. Or set out chairs." She bent over the dishpan. Could feel him staring at her back.

"Very well." He grabbed two chairs and hurried to the veranda.

"Missy, what's happened to ya? Where have ya put your smile and your song?"

She ha'nae realized Scotty was still there and had witnessed the scene. "Guess I'm feeling off this mornin'."

"Well, ya better get it fixed right soon. I don't care to see one of my boys hurt."

He was right. She dinna want to hurt Pete. "Aye, I'll fix it." She pushed aside her hurt feelings and the ache she felt at knowing she loved Pete but he might never love her. She wou'nae allow it to make her miserable or be the cause of Pete being miserable.

She finished the dishes and went out to join the others for the service. Pete sat in the same back corner as she had chosen the last two Sundays with his arm resting across the back of an empty chair. At the uncertainty in Pete's expression, she dismissed the last of her resentment. They were married and she meant to make the most of it. Why not enjoy what he offered?

Smiling in a way that made her eyes sting, she sat at his side.

He touched the shoulder farthest from him. "Hi, again."

She smiled up at him, almost overcome with love for this man. He was hers even if he'd wanted to wed another.

He shifted his leg so their thighs pressed together. A thrill ran up her spine at this little intimacy. But this morning she'd stuffed the letter into the pocket of this dress. The page crackled, reminding her of its presence and the words it contained.

It wouldn't be easy to forget the letter that lay between them.

FOR THE PAST SIX DAYS, Pete had looked forward to his homecoming. She'd be so glad to see him, she might forget the others and throw herself into his arms. He'd take her walking and they'd talk of what they'd done in the past week. And they'd kiss a time or two. Or more to make up for the days he'd been away.

Instead, she seemed less than eager to see him. At first, he put it down to being self-conscious in front of the others. When she sat beside him for the church service, shoulder to shoulder and leg to leg, he relaxed. It was as he thought, simply awkwardness.

He struggled to concentrate on John's words as he led the service. As soon as the final 'Amen' was spoken, he turned to Eva. "Shall we go for a walk?"

She looked toward the door. "I have to see to the meal."

Fine. He could understand her wanting to make sure everything was as it should be for the usual gathering. And he followed the other men down to the site of the future schoolhouse. It barely registered that little had been done since last week. Stakes had been driven in the ground to mark the perimeter. Adam had begun to dig a trench for the footings.

He looked back to the house. The women and children congregated there. He didn't see Eva. He'd have been able to pick her out by her red hair.

He sighed. Back in the kitchen, of course. But it was what she had agreed to.

A little later, Scotty banged the dinner triangle to signal time to eat and Pete hurried back to the house, anxious to see Eva.

She stood at the stove, watching the doorway. As soon as he stepped inside, she looked away.

A shiver snaked up his back. Something was wrong. But he couldn't imagine what.

He intended to find out before the day was over and whatever it was, he'd make it right.

A walk after dinner would give him a chance. Only she had to clean the kitchen. And then Sam said one of the horses was acting strangely and the men all trooped out to see what was wrong. Turns out the poor beast had a thorn in his hoof which was easily fixed.

The job done, the men each headed toward their homes.

Pete did the same. He stepped inside an empty room. John and Maude's voices came from the sitting room. He had no desire to disturb them. There was only one person he wanted to see. He looked out the windows. Where was she?

The day was almost gone and somehow they'd missed each other. He had long since decided it was intentional on her part and spoke to John, asking if he could stay at the ranch this coming week.

"The boys already talked to me. They all agreed you should be the one to stay."

Pete wondered if they'd sensed the strain between him and Eva and were hoping he could remedy the situation if given more time. He certainly hoped so. "Thanks. That's good of them."

"Maude and I have been thinking that it's not good for one of you to have to take care of me. Things have changed with all of you married."

Pete didn't point out that he alone didn't have his own home because he planned to stay in the big house. "John, we owe you at least that much."

John waved away his protest. "No one owes anything. But Maude and I are praying we'll find another solution. It's not that I need that much help."

"Of course you don't." Pete thought of the times John ran into problems with his chair or needed extra help when he wasn't feeling well. But what would become of him and Eva? He'd promised her a home here, in the big house. He didn't like to think he'd have to break his promise to her. Not that there were people lined up in the laneway seeking the job of taking care of John.

John might have read his thoughts. "Remember Maude found six young men and trained them to be cowboys. Then she set out to find wives for all of you. There's not much that wife of mine can't accomplish if she puts her mind to it."

Pete didn't point out that they'd all managed to find wives on their own. Who knows, but that Maude's plans might have started things moving? He certainly knew that John and Maude's prayers could move mountains.

Despite his desire to talk to Eva, the day passed and he'd not found a chance. Mostly because Eva managed to avoid him.

When the others left and he didn't, he couldn't mistake the look of surprise on her face. He prayed he didn't also see disappointment.

He helped John into bed. When he left the room, Eva was gone. Hoping she'd gone upstairs, he clattered up the steps.

She jumped when he entered their bedroom. She'd been staring out the window.

He closed the distance to stand beside her. "Eva, did something happen?"

"No. Why do ya ask?"

He knew she tried to sound innocent, but he heard a note of caution in her voice and was convinced that something had indeed happened.

"All week I looked forward to returning. Thought I'd get a welcoming kiss. Instead, you shy away from me."

"'Tis only that I was nervous about making the big meal and all."

"You did very well. The meal was excellent."

"Thank you."

He waited, giving her lots of time to say more, but she remained silent, looking out the window.

"Eva, there's something wrong." He gave her a moment to tell him but nothing. He tried coming at it from a different direction. "I remember the promise you made when we married. You said if there was a problem you would tell me so we could work it out. That's all I'm asking."

When she continued to stare out the window, his heart thudded to his feet. What had he expected? Nothing was forever when it came to people and their feelings. Hadn't he learned that in so many ways? So many times? Adopted and returned. Taken by family after family and returned. Even corresponding with Trudy and having his offer of marriage rejected. Still, he thought things would be different with Eva. He'd opened his heart to her, let her past his barriers.

Why should he be surprised that she didn't want what he had to offer?

15

It bothered Eva that she'd avoided Pete all day. But she was afraid she'd blurt out everything in front of the others. Now was the time to confront what she'd learned.

She moved toward the wardrobe, needing to be able to face him but not reach him. "I found this." She took the crumpled paper from her pocket and handed it to him. "You were planning to marry another. I have ruined your plans."

"No, that's not how it is." He took a step toward her, but she held up a hand to stop him.

"I read it. You asked her to marry you."

"That's true. You have to understand that it was what Maude and John wanted. We'd written back and forth a few times. She seemed a willing person. Said she'd always wanted to move west. Get away from her many interfering family members. I told her we were a large group too but she said it would be different with them not knowing every scraped knee and spilled cup of milk." He looked down at the page in his hand. "I wanted her to know what to expect from me. I wrote this page over, making sure she understood I didn't know my family or my heritage and that my skin was darker than most."

He swallowed audibly, then met her eyes.

She read in them a pain she'd seen before but stopped herself from offering the comfort she'd offered on those other occasions.

"She wrote back and said she found it unacceptable to marry someone who might be carrying foreign blood."

Eva wanted so much to hold and comfort him but... "So I am yer second choice?"

"No, Eva. I thank God that He stopped me from marrying Trudy and led me right to you. I thought—" He stopped. "Eva, I think we belong together like this." He clasped his hands. "You belong here." He waved his hand to indicate the entire room and maybe more. "And here." he pressed his palm to his chest.

"Ya don't regret marrying me?"

"Not for a minute." He opened his arms in welcome and she went right in. They hugged for a long time as she let her fears and uncertainties fade away.

She sighed.

"Something else bothering you?"

She could not keep the truth silent. "Aye. I want a home and children."

He leaned back, his eyes wide with shock. "What about our agreement?"

She gave a laugh that was as mocking as amused. "The honesty part or the marriage in name only part?" She didn't give him a chance to answer. "Because I'm being honest, but I will keep my promise to you. I will not regret anything, but it hurts to see the others with children and know we will not have any."

"Grace and Mike don't have children."

"They're hoping for some." Tears leaked out. "Dinna mind me. I'm feeling sorry for myself."

"Eva?"

But she hurried to the next room to prepare for bed and crawled under the covers while he went to wash up and change.

He slipped into bed.

Longing for things she couldn't have, she reached toward him knowing he was just out of reach but her hand touched his. Aye, was'nae he reaching for her too?

He gently tugged her toward him. "You're welcome to join me."

She needed no second invitation and she crawled into bed beside him.

"We can change our agreement anytime you want," he said.

"Aye, but only if you want."

"Eva, surely you've guessed that I love you."

One sob choked out. She quelled her tears. "I love you with everything I have and am."

He kissed her. His kiss deepened.

Their lovemaking was sweet. Everything she'd ever dreamed of. To love and be loved, to know and be known. Her heart flooded with joy. She was so blessed.

T‍HE NEXT MORNING, she practically danced down the stairs and prepared breakfast with joy bubbling in her heart. She didn't have everything she'd dreamed of, but she had something she hadn't thought possible—Pete's love.

Scotty entered and took the cup of coffee she handed him. "Nice to see ya happy today. I dare say you and Pete mended yer fences."

She laughed. "I suppose we have."

Pete came down the stairs, paused in the doorway to smile at her, then went to help John. Eva understood that her husband owed the older couple so much and would be loyal to them all his life. She cou'nae help but admire him for that even though it meant they would live here.

Pete's love for her made the sacrifice easy.

The following days became a pleasant routine. Despite the work in the house, Eva had time to spend an hour or two with Pete after dinner if he wasn't busy. She looked at the pile of lumber meant to become a schoolhouse and grinned. It seemed no one was overly eager to get the building up. Mr. George and his wife, Ilsa, had attended the last two Sunday services and Eva had overheard John talking to Mr. George from the store about having a work bee but nothing had been finalized.

Eva enjoyed evenings spent with Pete the most. They would walk and talk, or go to the bench and sit together holding hands and kissing. She had promised herself to never again speak of wanting a home of her own and children. So they talked of other things. The ranch. The cows. The others at the ranch. The approaching winter season. The need to get the root vegetables dug and into the root cellar.

"We could have snow any day," Pete said. "Early storms aren't unusual. The snow won't last this early though."

"I too am familiar with sudden storms. Winter or summer."

He held her close. "Our love will keep us warm."

She laughed at his optimism and kissed him.

THE NEXT DAY, Pete drove the wagon to the house and hurried in. He looked at her. "Maude has decided I need to go to Logan Crossing for supplies. You want to come?"

"I'd love to." She glanced at the bread dough rising and the cookie dough ready to bake. "But I can't. I have all this to attend to."

"Can't Scotty do it?" Or Maude? Hadn't they done all this before Eva came?

"'Tis my job and I will finish it." She kissed him. "I'll miss you. Come back soon."

He was disappointed she couldn't accompany him, but he also admired her for being conscientious. "I'll rush back to you."

"I'll be here waiting."

He kissed her again, then hurried to the wagon. What was so important on the list that Maude gave him that it couldn't wait until tomorrow? But Maude had been insistent.

A little later he drove up to the store in Logan Crossing and hopped down to take the list inside for Abner and Ilsa to fill.

He greeted them. A young man stood by the counter, his hat scrunched in his hands.

"I'm so glad you came today," Ilsa said. "This young man needs a home and the first place I thought of was the Circle A. Pete, this is Leo Johnson. Leo, this is Pete."

Leo held out his hand, grinning from ear to ear. "Hi, you the people Mama told me about?"

Pete's eyebrows went up. "I don't know." He looked to Ilsa for help.

"Leo's mother died. He has no family—"

Leo interrupted. "Mama said God would send me a family. I will be a big help. I can take care of people. You could ask my mama." A confused look came over Leo's face. "Guess you can't 'cause she's dead."

Pete studied the young man before him. He had an open eager expression of someone who saw life with nothing but hope. Leo's manner of speech gave Pete to think the young man was like a boy back in the orphanage who stopped growing mentally. Pete had liked the boy. He didn't have a mean bone in his body.

"How old are you?" he asked. It was impossible to guess, but the boy was big. He stood eyeball to eyeball with Pete.

"Leo is sixteen. A grown-up boy. Mama said so."

Abner had taken Pete's list and was gathering up items while Ilsa stayed with Leo and Pete.

"I'm hoping you'll take him to the ranch," Ilsa said. "I can't think of a better place for him."

Abner packed a box with the supplies and took it to the wagon.

"Leo, would you like to go to the ranch with me? You'd be welcome." Maude and John's door was always open.

Leo nodded. "I go with you. Mama said God would send someone to help me."

"Where're your things?"

Leo pointed to a bulging sack. He hoisted it to his shoulder and accompanied Pete to the wagon.

Leo talked all the way back to the ranch. Told

how he took care of his mama as she grew weak. Told how he couldn't stay in the house where he'd always lived. Following his mama's instructions, he'd gone to the first man he saw with a wagon and asked for a ride.

"Why did you get off at Logan Crossing?" Pete asked.

"I just did. Thought Mama would want me to."

A little later, Pete pointed to the ranch ahead. "That's where we're going."

Leo leaned forward. "It looks nice." He chewed his thumbnail. "Don't do that, Leo," he said. "You'll be fine. God will take care of you just like He always has."

Pete guessed Leo repeated words he'd heard his mother speak.

They pulled up in front of the veranda.

Maude was on her feet, looking at his passenger.

"This is Leo," Pete said. "He needs a home."

"Leo, you've come to the right place." She looked up at Pete. "I knew there was a reason to send you to town today."

Leo joined her on the veranda.

"This is my husband, John."

Leo shook John's hand. "Mama said there was someone who would need my help."

John laughed. "What did I tell you about Maude getting things done?" he asked Pete.

"It's God's doing," she said. "All I do is pray."

Leo was so eager to help that Pete didn't get a

chance to take the crate from the back. Leo hurried to do so.

"Where I take it?"

Maude led him inside.

Pete followed, looking past the pair for Eva. His heart sighed when she smiled at him.

Leo set the box down to shake hands with Eva. "I am here to help. Mama said you needed me."

Eva blinked then chuckled. "'Tis nice to have a cheerful helper."

Leo took things from the crate and waited until Eva told him where to put them.

Maude made shooing motions toward Pete. "Tend to the horses."

Pete backed away. He didn't turn until Eva met his gaze and smiled again.

He put away the horses and wagon, then joined John on the veranda. Neither of them spoke, though Pete wondered what having Leo here meant for his future. His and Eva's.

It didn't take many days for Pete to learn the answer to his question.

Leo was the first one down in the morning. He had coffee brewing by the time Pete and Eva descended. And handed them each a cup full of the fragrant liquid. Scotty liked the boy and welcomed him into the house. On the third day, the kitchen was empty, though the aroma rose from the coffee pot. The murmur of voices came from John and Maude's room. One of the speakers was Leo.

Wondering what was going on, Pete headed for the room. He stopped just inside the door. John was dressed and sitting in his wheelchair.

"Leo helped me," John said.

"I do a good job?" Leo asked.

"Couldn't ask for better."

Leo beamed at John's praise. "Mama said someone would need me." He pushed John's chair from the room, then allowed John to make his own way.

Pete hung back. He wasn't sure how he felt about being replaced.

Maude touched his arm. "I want you and Eva to be free to have your own home. You both deserve it."

"What about helping you and Scotty?"

"Oh, poof. I think we can manage. I've discussed it with the others and we've decided it's only fair for each of them to take turns helping on Saturday to prepare the Sunday feast."

They had reached the kitchen and the conversation ended before Pete could point out that there wasn't a house available for him and any building that took place would be to erect the schoolhouse.

That night as he and Eva lay side by side he told her of John's announcement. "John thinks he won't need me or any of the others now that Leo is here."

"Are you disappointed?"

He had to think a minute. "Guess maybe it feels a

little like events in the past."

"Och, no. No one is rejectin' ya or sendin' ya away. Did John say why he feels this way?"

"He says he wants you and me to have our own home."

She lay very still.

"Eva, are you disappointed?"

"No. But 'tis too much to hope for."

"Of course it's not. Isn't it what you want?"

"Aye, but I have prayed for God to take away that longing."

He chuckled. "What better way than to fulfill your desires?"

"Aye. 'Tis so." She was quiet a moment, as if mulling over what she'd learned. "'Tis a nice thought, but are we going to live in the schoolhouse once it's built?"

"I don't know. I'll talk to John about it when I feel the time is right."

But Sunday came. Abner and Ilsa attended the service and John picked a date for the building bee to put up the schoolhouse. Next Saturday.

Pete would not ask about a place for him and Eva until after that. He glanced at the sky. Winter would soon be upon them. Their house might have to be put off until spring.

He'd planned to stay in the big house with John and Maude, so why was it suddenly so important for him to have his own home with Eva?

Winter meant long hours at home and he wanted to share them with Eva alone, sitting by the fire, reading together, holding each other freely.

SATURDAY MORNING, men and wagons descended on the Circle A just as dawn lightened the sky.

John had been up an hour, eager to get started.

Abner drove one of the wagons and John directed him to a spot past Sam's cabin, a distance from where the school was to be built.

Pete followed the wagon, Leo and John beside him. "Why is there more lumber and why is Abner unloading it there?" Pete asked.

"It's for a house for you and Eva." John laughed at Pete's surprise. "Go help unload the wagon."

In a state of shock, Pete did as he was told. By the time the wagon was emptied and moved away, a crowd of people had gathered. Men and women and children. Eva came to his side.

"Do you know what this is?" he asked her.

"If I heard right, 'tis our house." She laughed. "Our house." She threw her arms around him, hugged him, and kissed him in front of the whole works of people.

And he didn't mind one bit.

What more could he ask for? A house which they would turn into a home and the love of a woman like Eva.

EPILOGUE

Eva stood in the middle of her house. The work bee had put it up in one day. When she asked about the schoolhouse, John said it was next on the list.

She and Pete had spent days finishing the interior. She hadn't felt there was any rush to complete the work as each day spent working side by side with him had provided so much pleasure.

The others had provided furniture and bedding. She'd hung her mother's sampler over the kitchen table. Eva had spent hours poring over a catalog and then ordering dishes, pots and pans, and other supplies. 'Twas a pleasant surprise to learn that Pete had a sizeable amount of money hidden away.

"Wages," he'd explained. "Maude and John always paid us for our work."

She'd purchased fabric for curtains at the store and yarn for knitting.

The new cookstove had proven to work perfectly and the meal was ready. Their first meal together in their new house.

Booted feet banged on the step and she hurried to the door, pulling it open. "Welcome home," she said.

Pete stepped inside, kicked the door closed, took her in his arms and kissed her soundly. "Nice welcome."

She laughed. "Let's make it a tradition."

He kissed her again. "I can agree to that." He held her as he looked around the room. "You know I never dreamed this was possible. In fact, it seemed so impossible, I never admitted to myself that it was what I wanted. A home of my own and a wife to love me."

"And children," she added.

"In time, I hope."

She cupped her hands over his cheeks. "In May."

He blinked. Opened his mouth and closed it again. Swallowed audibly. "Are you saying…?"

"Pete, my love, we are going to have a baby in May."

He hugged her, swung her off her feet, and danced across the floor. "You are amazing."

She laughed. "I dinna think I did it on my own. Grace is going to have a baby about the same time. But dinna ya be telling anyone until she or Adam says so."

"Come." He led her outside and put his arm around her. "Hello, everyone," he yelled at the top of his lungs.

Doors up and down the line of cabins flew open. Even those at the big house heard him and stood on the verandah.

Pete waited until everyone had stepped from their homes. "Eva and I are going to have a baby in May!"

There came clapping, cheering, and whistling.

Adam hollered. "Quiet down. I've got some news as well. We're going to have a baby too."

More cheering, clapping, and whistling.

Pete and Eva withdrew to their kitchen. She set out their meal. Although the food was excellent, she hardly tasted it. Her insides were too full of joy.

"I have everything I dreamed of," she said.

"I have more than I dreamed possible."

Their kiss said that dreams do come true.

ALSO BY LINDA FORD

Historical Romance

Love on the Western Trail

Renewed Love

Rescued Love

Reluctant Love

Redeemed Love

Romancing the West

Jake's Honor

Cash's Promise

Blaze's Hope

Levi's Blessing

A Heart's Yearning

A Heart's Blessing

A Heart's Delight

A Heart's Promise

Sunny Ridge, Montana

Rodeo and Juliet

Glory, Montana

Loving a Rebel

A Love to Cherish

Renewing Love

A Love to Have and Hold

Cowboy Father

Cowboy Groom

Cowboy Preacher

Rancher's Bride

Hunter's Bride

Christmas Bride

Love on the Santa Fe Trail

Wagon Train Baby

Wagon Train Wedding

Wagon Train Matchmaker

Wagon Train Christmas

Dakota Brides series

Temporary Bride

Abandoned Bride

Second-Chance Bride

Reluctant Bride

War Brides series

Lizzie

Maryelle

Irene

Grace

Wild Rose Country

Crane's Bride

Hannah's Dream

Chastity's Angel

Cowboy Bodyguard

Contemporary Romance

Montana Skies series

Cry of My Heart

Forever in My Heart

Everlasting Love

Inheritance of Love

Copyright © 2020 by Linda Ford

All rights reserved.

No part of this book may be reproduced in any form or by any electronic or mechanical means, including information storage and retrieval systems, without written permission from the author, except for the use of brief quotations in a book review.

Made in United States
Cleveland, OH
28 February 2025

14769596R00146